D1534073

ImPerfecT cHemistry
By
marY fRame

Copyright © 2014 by Mary Frame
Cover and e-book design by Regina Wamba of
MaeIDesign and Photography www.maeidesign.com
Line editing by Haestella. Any errors contained herein
are likely the result of the author continuing to change/edit
after the line edits where completed.

This book is a work of fiction. The names, characters,
places, and incidents are products of the writer's imagination
and have been used fictitiously and are not to be construed as
real. Any resemblance to persons, living or dead, actual events,
locales or organizations is entirely coincidental.
All rights are reserved. No part of this book may be
used or reproduced in any manner without written permission
from the author.

Frame, Mary,
Imperfect chemistry /

[2014]
▓▓▓▓▓ ██████████
sa   12/04/14

For my husband.
For being my perfectly
Imperfect
match.

Chapter One

*I believe that a scientist looking at nonscientific
problems is just as dumb as the next guy.*
—Richard Feynman

There are many theories that attempt to explain why humans cry in response to heightened emotions. One states that weeping serves as a signaling function, letting other humans know the emotional condition being experienced with the hopes of contriving an altruistic response in the viewer. Another theory is that crying serves a biochemical function, releasing toxins from the body and reducing stress. Some scientists have found that tears may contain a chemosignal, and when men sniff women's tears, they display reduced levels of testosterone and sexual arousal.

None of these theories explain why I, a twenty-year-old female, experience extreme anxiety and a desperate desire to get as far away as possible when people cry in my general vicinity.

"Are you even listening to me?"

Today's client is Freya Morgan, a sophomore at the university, who recently dissolved a relationship. She's pre-law, and her file indicates a fairly high GPA. I have hopes she will be more logical than emotional. She hasn't cried yet, but I'm 83% certain she will. Studies have shown that women cry thirty to sixty-four times per year. That's approximately once every twelve days, on the low side.

"Yes." I glance at my notes. "You engaged in coitus with your partner and then he stopped communicating with you."

She sits up slightly from the position she threw herself into when she entered the room, lying across the small sofa, and offers me a frown that puts a wrinkle in her forehead. She's shorter than me, small enough to lie down on the couch that's only about five feet long.

"Does that mean he went down on me? Because that's not what we did. I mean, we did that, too, but that's not what I said."

"Coitus is sexual intercourse. I believe what you are referring to is cunnilingus."

"Right." She nods after a small hesitation and then lies back down with a gusty sigh. "Where was I?"

"He stopped communicating with you."

"Yes!" She punctuates the word with a finger thrust in my direction although her gaze remains fixed on the ceiling above her. "But that's not all. When he wouldn't answer my texts, I went to his dorm and guess who was in there?"

I tilt my head, wondering, is that a rhetorical question?

It must be, because she's speaking again quickly. "Liz. Liz was in there and she was moaning and screaming like she was giving birth to a goat. One with horns."

"That's an interesting metaphor. Perhaps his advances were unwanted?"

She snorts a laugh. "She's been trying to bag him for months!" Her voice softens. "But I thought he was better than that. I thought I was better than that."

I'm amazed at how quickly she goes from indignant to depressed. I jot that down in my notes. *Bipolar?*

"Liz is a friend?" I ask.

"Hell, no, Liz is a total skank. She sleeps with anyone who has a pulse, guys, girls, whatever."

Whatever? I wonder what that encapsulates, but think it's best to stick to the topic at hand. "Okay. What about the gentleman in question, Cameron?" I clarify the name she stated earlier.

"Yes."

"Did you confront him regarding his behavior?"

Another heavy sigh. "Yes."

"And?"

"And he's a douchebag. He tried to deny it, but then I showed him the video."

"You obtained video of his transgression?"

2

"Yeah." She inspects her fingernails. "On my phone. They were so loud they didn't hear me open the door. I got the key from the RA."

"How did you..." I'm interested in how she accomplished such a feat, but it's not as important as why she's here in the first place. I have to stay on track. This exact topic was discussed with me previously by Duncan, the head of the psychology department and the person overseeing the progress on my experiment. Or lack thereof.

I didn't necessarily want to work in the peer counseling clinic, but one of the stipulations of the grant required that I put in the same number of hours as the graduate students. I was assured that my doctorate in immunology and pathogens more than made me suitable for the position, but since I started, I've been counseled on my own behavior nearly every day. I was told to use this as an opportunity to examine emotions and understand the underlying impetus of the passions people experience, since that is the basis of the grant: emotion as a pathogen, how emotion is transmitted from one person to another.

So far, it's not working.

I'm supposed to have an experiment proposal prepared by the end of next week and I don't even have a hypothesis. I have nothing.

If I'm unable to perform successfully, I will lose the grant, which means I will lose my place at the university where I've been studying since I was thirteen. Where would I go? My life is here. My family is here. This is all I've known.

Pulling myself away from negative thoughts that don't help my current situation in the least, and are therefore illogical, I clear my throat of the lump that's suddenly formed there and ask, "How did he respond when you showed him the video?"

"He said he didn't realize we were exclusive. Can you believe that bullshit?"

"Did you speak with him about exclusivity before the incident with Liz?" I ask.

"Well, no, but it was implied!"

There's silence for a moment and I try to think about a possible solution. One technique I've learned involves having the patient come up with the answer. If an individual becomes part of the problem solving, they are more likely to be engaged in the process.

"What do you think would make you feel better in this situation?" I ask. "Have you considered any possible solutions?"

Her eyes light up and she swings her legs around to place her feet on the floor, leaning towards me and lowering her voice an octave. "I've heard there's this guy on campus who will do anything for a fee. He runs some gambling thing and a drug cartel or whatever. Do you know who it is? I think he's, like, the son of a mob boss or something? I was thinking about hiring him to beat up Cameron."

I frown. "I've never heard of him, and I'm not sure violence is the answer."

She groans and covers her face with her hands. "You're right. I'm so stupid."

"You're not stupid," I assure her, but since I don't really know her, I'm not sure what else I can say to convince her of that.

There's another snort and a snuffle and since her face is still covered with her hands, all I can see are fingers and her shoulder-length light brown hair twitching as she shudders and squeaks. For a brief flickering moment I wonder if she's laughing, but no. She's crying.

Oh, no. Panicked, I stand up and reach for the tissue box on the coffee table next to my chair. I try to hand it to her but she's not looking at me, her hands are still over her face and her shoulders are shaking with muffled tears.

I have to get her to stop crying. I shuffle through the index of knowledge in my brain and pull out items at random.

"He's not worth it," I try.

She's still crying.

"You can do so much better."

Not helping. If anything, it's getting worse.

"By letting his actions affect you this way, you're giving up control of yourself to him. Don't let him have that kind of power. No one can hurt you unless you let them."

The crying is turning to sobbing.

"You know," I try, keeping my voice calm and monotonous, "there is an evolutional explanation behind the social patterns Cameron is exhibiting. Biologically, our urges are based on the continuance of the species. With this in mind,

4

logically, the male can inseminate multiple females with hardly any responsibility or time constraints, while females are required to endure a nine-month gestation period followed by nearly eighteen years of preparing their offspring to be self-sufficient. From a purely scientific standpoint, this explains both male and female behavior: why males feel it necessary to 'sleep around' like Cameron is doing, and why females are typically more selective. Women want someone who will take care of them and their progeny, hence the attraction to men with money and power. They also want someone with healthy genetic features that will pass onto their offspring, which explains physical attraction."

The snuffling slows down and her hands move away from her face, revealing red-rimmed brown eyes and a blotchy face. She sits up and takes the box of tissues I'm holding out in front of me like it will shield me from the torrent of emotions.

I breathe a sigh of relief. Duncan is wrong about my counseling style. Logic and reason can make people feel better. Not everyone needs coddling and emotional support. I sit down on the coffee table to place us at eye level.

She blows her nose before speaking and drops the dirty tissue on the couch. My eyes can't help but be drawn to it. Now I'll need to disinfect the couch.

"Understanding why cavemen felt it was okay to beat a woman with their club and drag her off to their cave while they went out and banged other cavewomen does not help me understand why my ass-wipe of a boyfriend cheated on me." She sounds angry. I drag my eyes from the mucous-filled Kleenex to her face. She looks angry, too.

This isn't good. I have enough things to worry about without having yet another complaint lodged against me.

"If he was an ass-wipe as you say, why are you upset? Aren't you relieved he will no longer penetrate you?"

"What?"

"If he was an ass-wipe as you say—"

"No, no." She shakes her head and eyes me warily. "I heard you, but don't you...haven't you ever liked someone who didn't like you back? Haven't you ever had your heart broken?"

"My experiences are irrelevant. I am here to help you." One of the books I read indicated that during an emotional session, physical contact can be helpful. Despite my personal inclinations to the contrary, I reach out and put my hand over hers. "It really is for the best. Plus, if he's engaging in sexual relationships with others, you run a serious risk of contracting a sexually transmitted or venereal disease. Have you been tested?"

She leans back slightly, pulling her hand out from under mine, eyes shifting to the side. "Um, no, but—"

"One in four sexually active people have herpes."

Her mouth drops open slightly. I've really gotten through.

"And that's nothing compared to human papillomavirus. Eighty percent," I continue.

"Okay," she says, nodding and putting the tissue box on the table next to me, her eyes focused on her hands. She takes a deep breath and meets my gaze. "You know what, you're absolutely right."

I smile. Of course I am.

"Thank you," she says and then glances behind me to the clock on the wall. "Thank you so much for all your help, and you've really been, uh, helpful, but I gotta go. I have statistics in ten minutes in the Geiger Building, and I really don't want to be late for that." She grabs her bag from the floor and fumbles it over her shoulder while stepping away from me and hurrying towards the exit. "Thanks again," she says, as she shuts the door gently behind her.

I look at the clock after she leaves. I have another two hours before the clinic closes. The whole session took less than thirty minutes. I briefly wonder if Freya was prevaricating when she left so abruptly, but then dismiss the thought. Why would she lie?

***

Duncan requested that I speak with him at the end of my shift. His door is shut, and I can hear the murmur of voices inside. I sit on the bench just outside his office and wait.

The voices inside escalate.

"They're unreasonable. My relationship ends through no fault of my own, and they're pissed at me. Like it's my fault. Like I've ruined all their plans for me and my future."

I don't recognize the voice speaking. It's male and deep.

"Do you think that maybe they're just concerned for you, and they want what's best?"

"That's the problem. They think they know what's best for me, but they don't. They aren't me. They don't have to live my life, I do. And if I try to argue or say anything against what they want, they threaten to disown me. It's all or nothing with them. They're completely irrational."

"Your father mentioned trouble with your classes?"

"Yeah. It's hard to stay focused when you're miserable, and being forced into a major you don't want," the voice says dryly.

Duncan responds, but it's too low for me to pick up.

The voices continue to murmur for a few more minutes, and then there's a shuffling and the door swings open. The stranger steps out and I realize that he isn't a stranger. It's my neighbor. Granted, I've never actually spoken with him, but I recognize him from seeing him coming and going on the other side of the duplex we both occupy.

He's tall, at least a head taller than my own five feet seven inches, and he has dark hair. I don't have a chance to make any more of an assessment on his appearance. His gaze slides over me like I blend in with the wall, and then he's stalking down the hall and out the main door.

Chapter Two

Learning must be experienced.
—William Glasser

"Have you come up with a proposal yet?" Duncan asks me, once we are alone in his office sitting across from each other.

I tense even though I expected this question.

"No." I shake my head.

He gives me an appraising glance. "You're supposed to have the hypothesis and proposal by the end of next week."

"I know."

He sighs. "That's not the only reason I called you in here, though."

"It's not?"

"Nearly everyone who sees you complains," he says.

"Nearly? There are some people who don't complain?" I ask.

"I was being nice. Everyone who sees you complains," he says.

That can't be true.

"But I've assisted some extremely stressed students. I am very good with time management and handling demanding and substantial workloads."

"You told one girl to stop speaking to her mother."

"The mother's expectations were too high for her daughter's capabilities, and it was affecting her concentration," I explain.

"Her mother is Professor McDougall."

I shrug. "So I was correct."

He leans forward, placing his elbows on the table and steepling his hands in front of his mouth for a second before removing them. "You have to listen and guide. Not criticize, or solve the problem right away. You have to help students find the solutions on their own. To listen and ask questions and show empathy so they are comfortable opening up. Guide them on the path, don't throw them down it. And don't even get me started on today's client."

This surprises me. "What do you mean? She seemed genuinely thankful."

"She was here to discuss a traumatic breakup, and you talked to her about biological urges and STDs."

"It seemed appropriate at the time."

He raises an eyebrow at me.

"Maybe I'm too literal," I concede. "But I don't see why that's a bad thing. You're very direct with me, and I appreciate it."

"Lucy, I'm blunt with you because that's how you communicate and I know you understand it. I've discovered it's the best way to share information with you. But I don't talk like this with other students in the program. I have to treat them all differently because everyone is different and everyone responds differently to constructive criticism. You're never going to get this project underway if you can't—at the very least—empathize with other people."

"I've read multiple books on human behavior, personality theories, body language—"

"Reading about people is not the same as understanding them. You have to understand more of life and what makes people tick, the motivation behind the behavior. You have to be able to relate to their experiences by experiencing them yourself."

I examine the wood-paneled wall and bookshelf behind him while I contemplate his words. I don't understand the pendulum of passions and angst that people my age seem to experience on a regular basis. It's difficult to conduct a study on something I can't even begin to comprehend.

How am I supposed to relate? My childhood was nothing like anyone I know. I've been studying at the university since I was thirteen. I'm nearly twenty-one. It's too late to catch up now. Although I suppose I could try to behave like other college students and see if the behavior will help me intuit the motivation behind it. At this point, I will try nearly anything to get this experiment started.

"You think I should consume illicit substances and engage in unprotected sex?" I ask.

He smiles. It's hard to see the motion of his mouth behind the graying beard, but his eyes crinkle underneath his wire-rimmed glasses. "No, Lucy, I just want you to experience life. You are a wonderful scientist, but you need to interact more. You need to understand how people tick, which can't always be explained with logic and quantified by science."

"I interact with other people. I've even been on a date, recently."

That's not entirely true. But I did go to dinner with an underclassman named Brad whom I tutored in calculus. Whether the interaction could be defined as a date is open to interpretation. But it doesn't matter. Duncan doesn't seem overly impressed.

"You spend most of your time with sixty-year-old scientists who are just like you and derive more joy from test tubes than from others. You need to get out there, open up, and find friends your own age who have diverse backgrounds and interests. You need to do things for fun."

"I have friends and interests." I'm still defending myself, but my protests sound weaker and weaker, even to my own ears.

"Archery once a month with your brother is great, but you also need friends that aren't family. Opening yourself up to new people and new experiences is a good way to start studying your own feelings. And if you start experiencing more emotions, you will find a way to study them."

I nod slowly.

"Look," he says, leaning back in his chair. His eyes roam around me, not quite meeting mine for a moment and I know he's uncomfortable, but he looks me in the eyes when he says, "You have no proposal for your grant, and working in the clinic isn't helping like we thought it would. We need to try something else. I'm going to put you on a temporary leave of absence until the end of the semester."

I open my mouth to argue, but he stops me with a hand. "I know you're worried about losing your funding. I'll talk to the board and see if they can extend the due date. This is temporary, Lucy. You need time to figure out what to do here.

You can come back in a couple months and we'll try again. If there's no progress on the study at that point, you will definitely lose this grant."

***

I'm failing. I can't believe it. I've never failed anything in my life. Well, that's not true. I did fail when I was twelve and conducting an experiment on DNA replication in E. coli the first three times, but I completed it on the fourth. I've always been able to finish something I've started, and this is not over yet. Although it is disconcerting that I've been pursuing this particular goal since last semester, nearly a year now, and it's not coming as easily as I imagined.

I'm walking through the quad enjoying the crisp fall breeze as I move towards the west end of the school. My duplex is located less than a mile away. It's an old building, a rare find in this area which has been built up in the last few years with apartments and student housing. I pass a few people heading to their evening classes. I have to step off the walkway to avoid a couple holding hands and taking up the entire path. When I stop, I pull my cell phone out of the side pocket of my bag and try to call Brad. I helped him, therefore he should help me. Besides, we're friends. Sort of. One date may be singular, but I'm pretty sure it means something.

The call goes straight to voicemail and I'm almost relieved. I hate speaking on the phone, but sometimes it's a necessary activity.

"Brad. It's Lucy. Please return my call."

I hang up and keep walking, pushing aside the self-doubt and uncertainty coursing through me. Surely he will help me. Our last interaction seemed to go okay; he even invited me into his dorm room after we shared a meal, an offer I politely declined.

I'm not sure exactly what I'm going to ask him. I need to feel emotions. Perhaps explore the typical college experience. Maybe I'll start there, ask questions about what it is, exactly, that college students do besides go to class. Surely that's a simple enough task.

I hear a loud, rhythmic pounding when I turn down the small alley that leads to my duplex. Someone is banging on the door. I quicken my steps, wondering if it's one of my brothers. When I get closer, I can see that it's not my door being pummeled into submission, it's my neighbor's. The same one I saw leaving the clinic not long ago.

I don't know very much about the student who lives on the other side of the duplex even though we've shared a wall for at least six months now, and our doors face each other. I've seen him a handful of times in the last few months coming and going, and I've seen quite a few other people coming and going, but I haven't paid much attention. Other than that and what I overheard today...I don't even know his name.

"Jensen! Come on, man, open up!" the stranger banging on the door yells.

Well, now I know his name.

"This is ridiculous! I love you man!"

And now I know his sexual preference as well.

Bang, bang, bang. "You're going to be really pissed at yourself if I die while I'm gone and you didn't even listen to me!"

I approach cautiously. He isn't necessarily psychotic, but this whole situation is odd. He has a slight accent that sounds Western European, Scottish or Irish or something. It's hard to tell when he's yelling, and I haven't heard enough words to be able to precisely determine the cadence.

Whoever he is, he's now resting his head against the door, his arms up on either side of him against the door frame. All I can see from the bottom of the steps that lead up to the porch is the back of a dark blond head, hair cut short, a gray pullover sweater and jeans. He's not very tall, only a few inches taller than me, but he looks fairly muscular under the sweater. I'm not sure I could defend myself if he turns violent.

He lightly thumps his head against the door a few times and says quietly, "I'm sorry. I'm sorry, but I'm not sorry. I fucking love her, you know, and if I have to choose, I will choose her every time."

I feel like an intruder. The emotion in his voice is raw and real, and it makes me exceedingly uncomfortable. I try to tiptoe up the stairs so he won't notice me, but the old wooden steps creak like they're being stabbed with each footstep and forced to remonstrate the torture being inflicted on them.

12

The guy at the door spins around and I hasten to my door, pulling my keys out to get inside as quickly as possible and to use as a weapon if necessary.

"Hello," he says.

I nod and keep moving, not making eye contact, instead focusing on putting the key in the lock. First the dead bolt, then the round door knob.

"I'm sorry about the theatrics," he calls to my retreating back, "I didn't mean to scare you."

And then I'm inside with the door shut and locked behind me. Scottish. He is definitely Scottish.

Once I'm alone, I relax. What is going on with my neighbor?

Chapter Three

*A failure is not always a mistake, it may
simply be the best one can do under the
circumstances. The real mistake is to stop
trying.*

—B.F. Skinner

By early afternoon the next day, I still haven't heard back from Brad. I tried calling him a few more times the night before and then sent him texts all morning at various intervals when I knew he would be out of class, but there has been no response. I start to worry that something is wrong with him. The one time we went to dinner, his phone was out on the table or in his hand at all times. I can't imagine what could be preventing him from responding since he appears to be inordinately attached to the piece of technology.

Luckily, I remembered most of his schedule from various conversations. Having a near perfect memory is useful at times.

He normally eats lunch a little later on Wednesdays, due to a lab class from eleven to one thirty, so at two I head to the cafeteria. I find him there, sitting in a booth with three other males that appear vaguely familiar.

"Good afternoon, Brad," I say, stopping next to their booth.

He's drinking a soda and chokes when I materialize next to him. "Lucy?"

"I apologize for startling you. I would like to speak with you privately."

"What are you doing here?" he asks after he stops coughing.

There is such a thing as a stupid question, but I didn't realize it until I tutored Brad. That's okay, though. He's not excessively smart when it comes to logic and math, but he does have a lot of friends and his social experience is superior to mine and that's all I care about at the moment.

"I would like to speak with you privately," I say again, a little bit slower this time.

"Listen, Lucy." Fully recovered from his choking fit, he leans back in the booth and places one arm along the back of the seat behind his friend. "You're a nice girl and I really appreciate you helping me with calculus, but I'm not your boyfriend."

"I never said—"

"You called me ten times last night," he interrupts. He doesn't look at me while he speaks; instead, he concentrates a majority of his focus on his friends who seem to be enjoying the conversation immensely.

"I only called—"

"And you've texted me all morning. This has to stop," he says firmly.

"It's only because—"

"We went on one date. And all you wanted to talk about were things I don't really understand. You gave me statistics on how drinking alcohol affects movement and brain activity or whatever."

"Gross motor skills and neural synapses." I finally get a sentence completed.

"Yeah," he says. "Whatever." He rolls his eyes and looks over at his friends again who are laughing behind their hands and shoving food in their mouths, pretending like they don't know what's happening right in front of them even though it would be impossible to ignore.

Brad runs a hand through his messy light brown hair, but the motion doesn't disturb the stylish disarray. "Look, it's just not going to work out. I'm sorry." He crosses his arms over his chest, a clear use of body language signaling the conversation is over, at least in his mind.

15

I could defend my actions. I could tell him of my intentions and that I did not believe him to be anything more than an acquaintance, but suddenly I don't want to waste my breath or my limited time.

Instead I nod. "Okay," I say. "Thank you for your honesty. I'm sorry I disturbed your lunch," I tell him and the rest of the table.

He looks a little surprised at my easy acquiescence and that's the last thing I see before I walk away. Unfortunately, I don't walk quickly enough to avoid hearing the chuckles and laughs that accompany my departure.

***

I head straight home from the cafeteria. I don't have anything else left to do for the afternoon since the only thing I have to work on is my pathogen study. Or non-study, as it seems to have evolved into.

Fortunately, for now, the grant will cover my rent and food stipend. I also receive a small monthly allotment due to royalties from articles I've published in science magazines. I don't have a car, so I don't have to worry about gas or insurance. My family usually takes me anywhere I need to go, but I don't go many places that aren't walking distance from campus other than my parents' house. They live about thirty minutes away, a little bit outside town, and one of my brothers usually picks me up and drops me off if necessary.

As I'm nearing home, my neighbor is parking his car—it's a classic car of some kind, black and shiny—in the one and only narrow parking spot next to our duplex. We end up in front of the building at the same time.

"Hello," he says, and motions for me to precede him up the stairs.

After yesterday, I find that I wish to know more about my neighbor. This is a new sensation for me. Not the being curious part—I always want to know everything about everything—but I tend to avoid social contact with anyone unless absolutely necessary and therefore make only polite overtures to ensure my mostly solitary existence. But now, I find myself genuinely interested.

16

"How are you?" I ask while walking up the steps. The words feel strange in my mouth. I'm not used to engaging in conversation without someone else holding the reins.

I glance back at him. There are slight gray smudges under his eyes and he's frowning at the ground in front of him. His face is covered in fine dark stubble, blurring the edges of his jaw and chin.

"Great," he says although he doesn't sound as if he means it. "Thanks." He doesn't sound as if he means that, either. His voice is deeper than I remember, but then, I've only spoken with him a couple of times and I was likely in a hurry and not paying attention to something as frivolous as the sound of his voice.

His response is interesting to me. Under normal social conventions he should return the question, but chooses not to. He's not interested in reciprocal conversation. The notion stings slightly. From what I've observed, my neighbor has an abundance of friends and his social skills exceed my own by a wide margin. And yet...Perhaps it's not me. Perhaps he's experiencing momentary depression or he's ill.

I don't say anything else because there's nothing more to say, and I'm back in my side of the duplex with the door locked behind me in seconds.

Once it's just me with my thoughts in the sparsely furnished space, I hang my backpack on the hook by the door and head to the computer. I've got to figure out how to get my experiment going and my life on track. I need to study emotions and now that Brad's out of the equation, I need a new plan.

There's only one person left whose emotions I can study.

Mine.

First, I need to narrow down my focus and figure out precisely which emotions are the most prevalent and important.

A few hours and one microwavable meal later, I've confirmed all my previous suspicions.

I went through all of the patient files at the clinic. I put all of the information into a spreadsheet that tracked the data and isolated the subjects to show the most commonly reported items.

There were a shocking number of eating disorders, and more than a few suicide threats, but all that took up only twenty percent of the data. The rest of the students, regardless of gender, visited the clinic to vent about their relationships. Every kind of association, from family to friendships to romance and sex. And sex seemed to be the winner. Premarital sex, sex before marriage, significant others cheating—I had experience with that yesterday—significant others being possessive and controlling, breakups, makeups, and nearly everything in between.

So this is it. I know more specifically what I need to learn about. I need to gain experience. I need to find friends and be more social. Experience lust...The thought makes me cringe a little. Was my suggestion to Duncan not too far off? Should I sleep around? The thought is less than appealing. Experience. I need experience with relationships. The words run around and around in my head.

I can find friends. That should be easy enough. Go to a social function, engage in conversation. How hard can it be?

As for sexual relations, maybe I can find someone to teach me about attraction, the chemistry that's not performed in a lab, along with all of the other factors that accompany serious relationships. I frown. That won't work either. Being taught would be just as effective as reading about it. I can't expect someone to explain it to me, I need to live it. But the thought of living it makes me feel queasy.

I'll just have to talk to people about their experiences. Maybe set up interviews and develop a questionnaire with the information I want. I can't go farther than that. Not yet.

I turn in my office chair around and around and finally stop it to face my front door.

Jensen. My neighbor.

I find him interesting. With the exception of our interaction today, he's a social creature. He understands people, better than me, and he's one of those males who oozes easy confidence and grace. From what I overheard in the clinic, he's recently experienced a breakup and he's having troubles with his family. All things I would like to know about. Maybe I can somehow get him to agree to an interview, or an experiment. Maybe both. It would be purely scientific and it would allow me to study him in social situations and perhaps learn through observation.

I shake my head. I don't know if that will work. I don't even know if he's in a relationship already or anything about him. As a matter of fact he might be homosexual, if the guy yelling how much he loved him the other day is any indication. Except, the stranger also murmured something about loving *her*, in which case...well, I'll never know unless I ask.

A quick glance at the clock above the stove reveals it's only eight o'clock. Surely early enough for a social call.

It's only ten quick steps from my door to his. I give the wood a brisk knock. I don't see any lights on from where I stand, but his car is still in the driveway. I'm sure he's home.

I knock again after waiting the customary minute or so, but still, no answer.

I return to my side of the duplex, only a little put out. Until I can run into my neighbor again, I need to do something else. Waiting is not a suitable option and it's not something I'm comfortable with, especially in this situation. The faster I can gain information, the more comfortable I will be.

One of the first steps to understanding a different culture is observation. I need to find an adequate place to observe humanity at its most basic level, in addition to widening my own socialization and experience.

I make a quick decision. A college party. That's where I'll start.

Chapter Four

A first visit to a madhouse is always a shock.
–Anna Freud

I suppose I'm lucky that it's the end of October and there are more than a few parties available for me to choose from. It takes only a few minutes to find a listing of the fraternity organizations online that are hosting Halloween celebrations, and since it doesn't really matter, I pick the one at the top of the list.

I've never been to a party before. Not like this. The largest social gathering I've attended was an applied physics conference that the university hosted last year, and this is nothing like that. For one, at the conference, people were fully clothed in items that covered every part of their body.

I've never felt so overdressed in my life. I generally don't care what I'm wearing as long as it's comfortable and functional. With that in mind, I dressed up—because the website specified this is a costume party—as a doctor. I borrowed a pair of scrubs and an old stethoscope from Dr. Freeland in the neurology department, but now I realize I would blend in more if I had arrived in my bra and underwear.

The fraternity house itself is a beautiful piece of mid-twentieth century architecture, a large brick building with Corinthian columns and dormer windows. The inside might be just as nice as the outside, but it's hard to tell. After I pay five dollars at the door for a red solo cup—even though I insist I won't be drinking anything more than water, or perhaps tea if it's available, which I am assured by the man in a toga at the door that it is not—I enter the building and am immediately surrounded in darkness, punctuated by flashing colored lighting.

I can hardly see anything in the front hallway except snippets of scantily clad bodies in the irregular blinking lights, and there's a lot of noise. The music is so loud and the lights are so distracting, I immediately head through the throbbing dancers towards the only thing that seems stable: the backyard.

It's cold outside; late October nights are generally ten to fifteen degrees above freezing. I'm glad I wore a long sleeve thermal underneath the scrubs.

For a second I just stand there and watch. People are milling about, talking and laughing, smoking and drinking.

What disturbs me the most after a minute of lurking in the doorway, is that everyone seems to be having a fantastic time, and I have no clue what to do with myself. Is something wrong with me?

I shake the thoughts away. Perhaps I need to be closer to the action.

I weave through the open crowd and stop when my eyes alight upon a familiar face.

Freya. The name comes back to me, the image of her file blinking into my mind. Freya Morgan, the girl I counseled for my very last session. She's dressed as a pirate, which makes her stand out a bit since she is wearing a jacket and tight pants with boots, and her body is mostly covered. There's an eye patch over one eye and a fake green parrot on her shoulder.

It's odd to see a familiar face amongst all this madness, and without quite realizing it, my feet take me in her direction.

She sees me coming, and recognition ripples over her face like a wave. She grimaces slightly before smiling.

"Hello," I say.

"Hey," she says. She's standing with another girl in a pirate costume with a wooden leg, and a guy dressed as a pink flamingo, his arms and legs covered in pink feathers.

"Well, this is awkward," she laughs. Her friends glance over at us briefly, but they seem to be having some kind of argument about food and they are very focused on their discussion.

21

"Is it?" I ask. I don't like being around all these people and having to engage in conversation, but that's not awkward. Right?

She takes a drink from her cup. "The last time I saw you, we talked about herpes."

Her friends stop arguing and stare at me.

"I'm sorry about that," I offer because it seems like the appropriate response, although I'm not really sorry. It was sound advice, after all.

"It's okay," she says. "You know, after I thought about it a little, I think you're right."

"Really?" I ask. Of course I am.

"Yeah. I mean, your bedside manner sucks, but the information was good."

"Herpes?" the pink flamingo asks.

"Don't ask," Freya tells him, waving her hand that's not clutching a red cup. "Guys, this is...what was your name again?"

"Lucy."

She introduces me to the flamingo whose name is Ted, and the other pirate whose name is Bethany.

"Why do you have a stuffed goat?" I ask Bethany. She's pretty under her pirate hat and fake beard. She has wild, curly blonde hair and blue eyes.

"That's Nigel," Ted says. "She brings him to every costume party. It's like a thing."

"Okay," I answer, not entirely sure how to respond.

"I need a refill!" Bethany declares before grabbing Ted's hand and yanking him off towards the keg.

"So what are you doing here?" Freya asks, after her friends are gone. "This doesn't really seem like your kind of function."

"It's not." I focus down at my sensible sneakers for a second and then back up at Freya. "I'm here because I've been dismissed from the clinic," I start to explain.

"Oh, no," she groans. She puts a hand on my arm. "Is this some, like, revenge thing? You're going to start following me around, infiltrating my life, and single-white-femaling me until I crack? Look, I'm sorry I complained about you, but I've been so upset about Cameron, I really wasn't myself."

"Revenge? No." I shake my head slowly, not quite following her train of thought. "And I'm not sure what single-white-femaling is. I'm here to learn more about behavior and emotions so I can continue work on the grant I was awarded last semester. It's not your fault. There were other factors leading to my removal."

"Well, that's a relief." She takes another drink. "What kind of emotions are you studying?"

I pause a moment to gather my thoughts before responding. "Primarily lust, attraction, sex and sexual encounters. My goal is to study my peers in an effort to discover the motivation behind these behaviors and be able to relate to them on a more personal level."

"Okay, okay, I gotcha." She points her finger at me. "Number one, stop referring to people as 'peers'. Number two, there's only one way to understand attraction, you have to feel it. You need to find someone physically appealing. Then, talk to them. If they're cool, the attraction increases. If they're jerks...well." She shrugs. "Sometimes the attraction still increases, but hopefully not."

I shake my head. "That doesn't make sense."

"Yeah, well love's a bitch." She takes a long drink from her cup.

Ted and Bethany return and now they each have two red solo cups.

"I'm telling you," Ted says to Bethany, arguing with his hands and causing beer to slosh out of both cups in a small wave onto the concrete patio, "reheating food you haven't eaten any part of is not leftovers."

"It is too!"

"Is not!"

"Oh, God," Freya says to me. "I apologize for their behavior in advance."

"What do you think?" Ted asks me.

I look from Ted to Bethany to Freya and then back at Ted.

"About what, exactly?"

"If you buy a meal, and don't eat any of it," Ted says, emphasizing the last three words. "And then eat the whole thing the next day...is it leftovers?"

I consider the question. "Well, the term 'leftover' implies something that was once a part of a larger amount, the remainder, if you will. So I wouldn't consider the situation you describe as leftovers."

"See! The nerd agrees with me."

"However," I add, "it would be day-old, twice-heated food."

"Yes!" Bethany hands one of her beers to Freya and hits Ted in the head with Nigel the stuffed goat. "Gross ass."

"Shut up."

"Very diplomatic answer." Freya lifts one of her cups towards me in recognition.

"Thank you?" I say uncertainly.

"I like you," Ted says to me.

"Okay," I say.

"Hey, guys, Lucy needs some help with something," Freya says.

"Oh yeah?" Bethany asks.

"She's doing this, like, research thing, and she has to learn about sex and stuff."

"That's a much abbreviated version," I say.

"Do you need to lose your virginity?" Ted asks, his flamingo head bouncing forward and backward with each word. "Because you really don't want to do that here."

"No, it's not that," I explain. "I'm studying relationships. I'm not really sure what I need to do, but I suppose it would be helpful to feel an attraction to someone, someone who hopefully returns the sentiment."

"Honey, what you need is a man," Ted says, placing a pink feathered hand on my arm. "A straight man," he clarifies, removing his hand gingerly.

"That's more or less accurate," I say.

"Well, do you have anyone in mind?" Bethany asks.

"Not really."

"Do you *know* any guys?" Freya asks.

"That depends on if you are using the word 'know' as meaning to be aware of through observation, or if you are using it to mean having a relationship with someone through spending adequate amounts of time with them."

"The second thing," Freya says.

"In that case, no."

"You are so screwed," Bethany says.

"No she's not!" Ted smacks Bethany on the rear end. "And that's sort of the problem." He chuckles at himself and Bethany mimics a drum roll.

They laugh and then Bethany turns to me, "What about the first definition? Is there anyone you are 'aware of through

24

observation,'" she uses her fingers to make air quotes, "that might fit the bill?"

"Perhaps."

"Who?" Freya asks.

"Do tell!" Ted encourages.

I pause for a second, watching their expectant faces before answering. "Jensen. I don't know his last name. It's possible he is a homosexual."

Ted squeals. "No fucking way! It's gotta be Jensen Walker, I don't know any other Jensens that go here and honey, I wish he was curvy, but that man's straighter than Bill Clinton, if you know what I mean." He nudges me in the side with his elbow.

I'm not entirely sure what he means. They talk so quickly and ask so many questions, I don't have time to process.

"How do you know him?" Freya asks.

"He's my neighbor."

There's a collective gasp. "You're kidding!" Bethany exclaims.

"Would it be considered humorous if I were?"

Ted erupts into giggles.

Bethany shushes him. "Why would you think he's gay?" she asks me.

I explain the occurrence I observed the other day when I came home, and how the man was yelling at his door. I don't relate what I overheard at the clinic because I don't feel it's ethical to discuss something that should have been private to begin with.

"Dude, that was totally Liam." Freya nudges Ted with her arm, causing him to spill more beer on the concrete patio. "Did he really say he loves her?" she asks me.

I look at all of their enraptured faces, an expression that took over the minute I started my story. "Do you know who and what he was talking about?" I ask. How is this possible?

Ted chugs the remaining contents of one of his cups, and then throws it over his shoulder. In the distance, a girl's voice yells, "Hey!" over the hum of the crowd, but it doesn't deter him. "So, the story is that Jensen and Chloe have dated since they were, like, toddlers, and over the summer she cheated on him with his best friend! They had sex in a hot tub at SAE." He smiles and nods knowingly.

"Then," Freya continues, "Jensen and Liam got into a huge brawl outside the Lombardi Building. I totally saw it."

"How do you guys know so much about this?"

"It's all over campus." Freya shrugs. "And Jensen is on a pre-law track, like me, so I hear stuff."

"Rumors are typically 80% false," I point out.

"Whatever brainiac." Freya rolls her eyes. "The point is Jensen Walker is single, and word on the street is there's been a line of ladies from here to the quad keeping his bed warm since Chloe vacated the premises. They've started calling him Law School Lothario. I have no doubt you have a shot at getting his help, if ya know what I mean." She winks and nudges Bethany with her elbow.

I frown. Hearing about him sleeping around decreases my interest. "I'm not sure," I say. "If he's sexually active, this might be a bad decision."

Freya wrinkles her nose at me. "Is this about the herpes thing?"

"Perhaps," I concede.

"You want your job back, right?" Freya asks.

"Well, yes, but—"

"No buts. You need to live a little! It's not going to kill you to have some fun," Freya says.

I mull over my options before saying, "Maybe I can ask him about his experiences instead and get firsthand accounts of what it's like to undergo that sort of heartbreak and why that triggered the need to engage with multiple partners. Maybe it's because he now feels emasculated and insecure about his manhood."

Ted snorts. "Having fun means doing more than interviewing man-sluts. You need to slut it up a little yourself, girlfriend. Look at you, you're like a crazy cat lady and you're only sixteen."

"I'm twenty," I correct him.

"Whatever."

"I'm not sure," I say, even though what they are suggesting is exactly what has been running through my mind. "But I'll consider it."

"Will you let us give you a makeover?" Ted asks excitedly.

"No."

"Damn."

"Why do you always have to be so stereotypically gay?" Bethany groans.

Ted gasps. "I am not!"

26

"Are too!"

"I like football," he says, placing his hand on his hip. "That's doesn't fit into your stereotypes, you bitch."

"It's true," Freya says to me. "And he's a Raiders fan if you can believe it."

I have no idea what she's talking about and the conversation dissolves into Ted and Bethany arguing over who is the bigger bitch, him or her.

I think I've reached my capacity for social interaction for the day.

"I have to go now," I say and turn away to leave.

"Wait!" Freya stops me with a hand to my arm. "What are you going to do?"

"I'll knock on Jensen's door tomorrow and ask him if he'll assist me."

What else would I do?

Her expression turns horrified. "You can't just proposition him out of nowhere like that!"

"Why not?"

"Well first of all, have you ever even talked to him?"

My mind races through the past six months he's lived in the duplex. I'd only seen him on a handful of occasions other than yesterday and usually avoided any type of interaction. "Once. The other day," I admit.

"Before you start your interrogation, maybe talk to him a little, get to know him a bit, and then ask for help."

"Okay." That actually makes sense. The questions I will be asking are very personal, and it would be good to have him as comfortable as possible so there's no risk of understating his answers. "Thank you."

I turn around again and walk away, but not before hearing Ted say, "She is so weird. I think I love her."

Chapter Five

Small minds are concerned with the
extraordinary, great minds with the ordinary.
—Blaise Pascal

The phone rings four times before there's an answer.

"Hello?" Her voice sounds groggy. Did I dial the right number?

"Freya?" I ask.

"Yes? Is this a telemarketer? Because I don't have any money to buy crap," she croaks.

"No, this is Lucy. We spoke last night. And we also spoke on Wednesday at approximately 1:35 p.m. in the peer counseling clinic."

"Yeah, sure I remember. What's up Luce?"

"I was wondering if I could ask for your advice."

"Uh, sure, sure." There's a rustling of fabric on the line as if she's sitting up in bed. "Wait, how did you get this number?"

"From your file at the clinic."

"Oh." Pause. "You went through my file?"

"It was necessary before your session. I have a very good memory."

Another pause and then, "Okay, shoot."

"You mentioned last night that I should form a friendly relationship with Jensen before propositioning him. I've thought over your advice and I think it's reasonable. What is the most expeditious way to accomplish this?"

"Um. Well, you could do something neighborly, like invite him to a party."

A party. I grimace before answering. "What if that's not an option? What else?"

"Let's see," she says. There's more rustling and movement on the line and then, "You could ask him for a cup of sugar or something. Don't neighbors do that?"

"What would I use the sugar for?"

"Why does that matter? I dunno, to make cookies?"

I consider this. "I could make cookies. Then after I make them, I could bring him some. That's neighborly, correct?"

"Sure."

"And this also affords two separate opportunities for conversation."

"Right," she agrees.

"Thank you for your time," I say, and hang up the phone.

***

I've always enjoyed cooking. It's a bit like science. You mix things together in a certain order in certain quantities to achieve the desired outcome.

I have plenty of sugar on hand, and although I hate being deceitful, it's one harmless white lie and it's the means to an end. I never considered myself particularly Machiavellian, but I'm willing to try nearly anything at this point. At about three o'clock, I head over to the neighbor's door and knock.

No answer. I'm fairly sure he's home because I can see his car, and I heard him entering his side of the building approximately an hour ago.

I knock again a bit harder and the door swings open.

"Hello," I say. This is the first time we've been face to face and not just coming or going. He looks better than the last time I saw him. The gray circles under his eyes are gone and he's slightly flushed, like he's been exerting himself recently. He's wearing a light brown shirt with dark smudges like he's been rubbing dirty hands on it. His fingertips are tinged with some kind of black substance. If his car wasn't sitting pristinely in the driveway, I would think he had been doing something mechanical.

Looking at the shirt makes me notice other things. Like I didn't realize his shoulders are so broad. He's attractive, in a conventional way. Although he has brown hair and brown eyes and that description seems rather dull and plain, his features are nice. He must have shaved recently. The scruff is gone revealing a patrician nose and strong jaw. His face is symmetrical. Humans find symmetrical features attractive because it's a sign of superior genetic quality and developmental stability.

He's not smiling. He looks rather brooding, but it's a good look on him.

"Can I help you?" he asks and I realize I've been studying him without speaking for an unknown quantity of time.

"Do you have any sugar?" I ask.

"No," he says before closing the door. He manages to eke out a quick "Sorry," before the door shuts gently in my face.

Well. That didn't quite go as planned.

**

I rack my brain for the rest of the evening on how to initiate a discussion with Jensen, but to no avail. Not knowing what to do is a foreign sensation for me, but in this case, I am completely out of my depth. I have no idea how to make friends. I don't socialize. The only people I have any type of relationship with besides my family is other students I tutor or lab with. And even then, it's never social, it's more professional.

For the first time in my life, I start to wonder about myself. What is wrong with me that this is so difficult?

The next morning, I decide to call Freya again. Maybe she will inspire another idea.

"Hello?"

"Freya?"

"Lucy. Why do you always call at the ass crack of dawn?"

I glance at the clock above my stove. "It's seven thirty. Don't you have class at eight?"

"Holy shit!"

Click.

"Hello?"

Two hours later I find Freya.

I'm leaning against the wall directly opposite the door when her class ends. She exits, speaking with another student. When she sees me, she says something to excuse herself and then heads in my direction.

She waves as she walks over, adjusting her bag. "If I didn't already know what a weirdo you are, this would totally creep me out."

"I need your help," I say.

She purses her lips and considers me for a moment. "I missed breakfast and I'm starving. I'll help you if you buy me some food."

"Okay."

We travel in silence to the cafeteria, mostly because Freya is walking so fast, I'm panting to keep up. Also, morning is a busy time on campus, and we have to weave in and out of the crowd of students heading to their classes to make it to the cafeteria.

She orders a large stack of pancakes with eggs and sausage and picks up a few single-serving boxes of cereal on the way to the register.

"Are you going to eat all that food now?" I ask as I swipe my card.

"No," she says around a mouthful of apple. "I'll save some for later. Starving college student and all that."

We sit at a booth and while she's shoveling food into her mouth, I tell her what happened yesterday when I knocked on Jensen's door.

"Are you sure you want to keep pursuing this? You're a cute girl and all, but this is Jensen Walker. He's like a bluefin tuna in a sea of canned albacore. The likelihood of catching him on your line is slim to none. I'm sure we could find you another guy to harass."

I hesitate for only a second, not sure I completely understand her metaphors before answering. "I'm sure. I'm not going to proposition him like you think I am. I'm going ask him questions. He's the perfect candidate to help me further my emotional education due to the conflict he's experiencing in his relationships. Plus, I think I might be attracted to him." Not to mention the fact that I'm not attracted to anyone, ever. But yesterday, when I was staring at him, and the fact that he's a bit of a mystery...

31

"You *think* you're attracted to him? You *think*? Honey." She wipes a bit of syrup off her mouth with a napkin and tosses it on the table, gazing at me with an intensity that would be frightening if she wasn't five foot nothing and her voice was less squeaky. "The man is a god. Wooden posts find him attractive. Dogs jump six-foot fences for the opportunity to hump his leg as he passes. You'd have to be dead or blind to not find him attractive."

I'm not sure I agree with her assessment. Is this what most people think of Jensen? I noted his features were symmetrical and he's conventionally handsome, but if I had known the female population held him in such high esteem I might have looked elsewhere. I may not understand most social conventions but I know when someone is out of my league, so to speak.

"What do I do now?" I ask her.

She finishes her last bite of pancake and grabs a flosser out of her bag and starts cleaning her teeth.

"Well, let's see." She throws the flosser on her plate after a moment. "You could lock yourself out of your house and use his phone to call the locksmith?"

I consider the possible consequences of this scenario.

"I'm not sure," I say. "I don't want to give him another opportunity to tell me no. Or what if he doesn't answer his door?"

She begins shoving the small cereal boxes into her bag along with some extra syrup packets and plastic forks she procured from the condiment counter. "Well, you're the brain here, what do you think?"

"I think I should just knock on his door and tell him what I want."

She gasps in horror. "No! Not that again!"

"Why not?"

"Because it's crazy." She finishes stuffing her bag and slams it on the bench seat for emphasis. "And he doesn't know you. He'll think you're a weirdo and he'll definitely say no."

I consider this. She's probably correct. I should listen to her since she has friends and likely knows what she's talking about, at least in comparison to myself.

Another thought strikes me, inspired by her suggestion. "What if he was locked out of his house and had to come to me?"

She raises her eyebrows at me. "How the hell are you going to pull that off?"

"I don't know. Yet."

She laughs. "Girl, you've got balls the size of Cleveland."

"Is that good?"

"It's badass," she says with feeling.

I'm still not sure if she's paying me a compliment, but I nod and smile. My mind is already contriving possible scenarios to put my plan into action.

Chapter Six

Ask an impertinent question, and you are on your way to the pertinent answer.
                                    —Jacob Bronowski

It takes almost a week of observation, watching out my peephole and listening for his car coming and going, along with carefully posed questions at various locales throughout campus that Jensen frequents. The time and effort is well spent on learning a few important things about Jensen Walker.

For one, there isn't a horde of females coming and going as I was led to believe.

There is one female, a tall blonde, that goes to his house occasionally, stays a few hours and leaves. I suppose she could be a girlfriend of some type, but he never leaves with her so the odds are likely they are not exclusive. The observation makes me feel better. The thought of being one amongst many isn't enticing. Perhaps Freya's rumors are wrong—which I find likely—or perhaps he went through a phase of sexual independence but has now moved on. That theory is much more appealing.

He also leaves the duplex to go to class, and I am able to obtain his class listing from the school registrar, but other than that, he's generally at home and he's generally alone. It's interesting. He moved into the duplex last semester and I seem to remember him having people over—not enough to disturb me excessively—but he was socially active. During the summer months, he was gone, but since this semester began, I don't recall seeing anyone over there except last week's visitor.

I know he has friends. In fact, when I trail him around campus, he's acknowledged or spoken to by approximately one out of every three people he passes. Despite this, his social calendar seems to be as sparse as my own.

The most important thing I discover during the week of observation is that every Sunday morning, he goes to get coffee from the stand that opens outside the library at seven o'clock. Even more important: he leaves his door unlocked. I'm not sure why he does this. It seems illogical to put your possessions at risk, even for a short time. If I were criminally inclined, this would be the perfect opportunity to sneak in and steal something of value.

The only variable I am unable to anticipate is whether he brings his phone with him. Looking out my window and through the peephole in my door isn't enough to ascertain whether he puts his cell phone in one of his pockets when he leaves. If so, he may be able to use that to call for assistance when he gets locked out.

But there's only one way to know for sure.

On Sunday morning, I set my alarm to wake me up at six thirty. Like the week before, he leaves his place at six forty-five on the dot. As soon as he rounds the corner at the end of our little alley, I bolt out of my house to his door, open it, reach inside and turn the lock then shut it again. I double check to make sure it can't be opened, before running back inside my house.

Then I wait.

Per my calculations, which I obtain by walking the distance myself, it takes six minutes and seventeen seconds to walk to the library from the duplex. On average, it takes two minutes thirty-four seconds for the employees at the coffee stand to make the drink and obtain cash for the purchase. That means I have at least fourteen minutes and fifty-one seconds of pacing. Longer if he walks slower or there are other's in line before him.

It takes fifteen minutes and forty-two seconds for him to return and I watch through the peephole as he attempts to open his front door and fails.

"What the—?" He tries a few more times. Finally, he puts his coffee on the railing that runs against the porch and pats down his pockets.

I almost hear his heavy sigh, seeing his shoulders heave slightly as he runs his hands through his hair in agitation.

Then he turns around and walks to my door.

Suddenly nervous—at least, I assume that's the emotion coursing through my system, it's the only thing I can think of to describe my abruptly rapid heart rate and sweaty palms—I bolt down the hallway away from the door as he approaches, like he might sense me hovering on the other side. Why am I so panicked? No one is crying. My life isn't in danger. The emotion is irrational and confusing.

He raps out a brisk knock. I try to take my time and pretend I was in the back and am now moving towards the door.

I open it slowly.

"Hey." His hands are in his jean pockets under a thick sweater and he rocks back slightly on his heels. "I seem to have locked myself out. Can I use your phone?" The words create fleeting puffs of clouds in the cold morning air.

"Just...one second," I say, finger in the air.

Then I shut the door on him.

What am I doing? I'm supposed to invite him in, come to his rescue, have a conversation, and get friendly. But I just...I can't. I hate this deception. This isn't me, and Freya might be right, but I just can't do this. Not this way.

I race to my bathroom and grab a bobby pin. When I return and open the front door, Jensen is leaning on the railing with his coffee cup in hand, looking down the alley.

I clear my throat and he turns.

I show him the bobby pin. "I'll just...uh." This is ridiculous. I'm never inarticulate.

Instead of continuing to speak in stilted phrases, I move to his door, kneeling in front of it and sticking the bobby pin into the lock. It only takes a few seconds to spring the pins and the door swings open.

"There you go," I say, stepping back.

"Wow." He seems surprised. "Thanks. How did you do that?"

"It's fairly simple if you understand the basic locking mechanism."

"All right." I try to decipher the look he gives me, but I don't excel at translating facial expressions. I think it's a cross between confusion and uneasiness.

"It's a good thing you didn't engage the dead bolt," I say. "It's harder to flip."

"Right." He gives me a half smile that seems forced. "Thanks again." He steps by me and through his doorway.

"Wait!" This is it. This is the only opportunity I'm going to have and I'm going to take it. I'm going to do this my way.

"Yeah?"

"Can I ask you a question?"

"Um, sure."

"It will take a few minutes. Do you have a few minutes now?"

"I...guess." The reluctance in his voice is nearly palpable.

I step forward, but he steps towards me at the same time and shuts his door behind him, bringing us too close together. I step back.

"Can we talk at your place? My place is...dirty," he says.

"Okay," I say and lead him to my side of the building. Once inside, I usher him into the small living room and motion for him to sit on the couch.

He sits and I pace in front of him, gathering my thoughts.

I stop and face him. "You see, I'm a scientist." I start pacing again. I'm not sure why, but I still feel nervous, and the movement keeps me calm.

"Okay." Now he sounds confused, but I suppose it's better than reluctant.

"I have a doctorate in microbiology, with a focus in immunology and pathogens."

"Wow. Really?" That seems to have captured his interest. It usually does, which is why I don't share the information regularly. I don't want people to be interested in me.

"Yes. I've been attending this university since I was thirteen, and I graduated from the doctorate program last year."

"That's...oh, I've heard of you."

I stop pacing again and face him. "You have?"

"Yeah, my dad's a professor here."

I sit on the small coffee table and face him.

"Professor Walker," I say, the name coming together in my mind and conjuring a picture of the man in question. "He's a wonderful lawyer," I add. I've never taken any of his classes, and we haven't officially met, but he's a large contributor to various departments. He teaches classes at the law school and he owns a prestigious firm in town.

"That's not why I wish to speak with you. You see, I was given a grant last semester to study emotional pathogens. The idea is that emotion is transmittable, like a virus or cold. The problem is that I don't really understand emotions."

"You don't?"

"No." I shake my head. "Which means, I'm supposed to be testing a theory and I don't even know where to start. I'm not good with people," I say. I stand up again and resume my nervous pacing. "I never have been good with people. I've never been very good with emotions in general," I tell him. "And because of that, I need to learn."

"Okay," he says again, more uncertainly this time.

"My...friend," I guess that's what she is, I think rapidly while I begin pacing again, "My friend Freya, you see, she told me you've slept with half of campus. The female half."

"Excuse me?" Oh no, he doesn't sound happy. Maybe I should have left that part out.

"No, that's not what I meant. I meant to say, I won't be able to pursue this course of study unless I learn more about people and relationships."

He's still staring at me, his mouth slightly agape with an indecipherable expression on his face. Well. I have nothing to lose now.

"You see, after conducting statistical research, I discovered that the emotion most relevant to people in general involves relationships. Sex, love, lust, all of that, and I have very little knowledge about these things. But if this is what most people are experiencing, it's what I need to study."

He stands. "Look, I'm not sure what you've heard from your friend, but I am not some kind of gigolo." He turns towards the door.

Oh, no. This is no good. Why did I say that? Why am I having such a hard time explaining myself to him? It was easy enough with Freya.

I move in front of him before he reaches the door. "Wait, no. That's not what I'm asking."

"I don't want to pay you for sex." That much is definitely true. "I want to understand human emotions which include attraction. I want you to teach me everything you know about it. You don't have to do more than speak. I assure you I will keep everything in the strictest confidence."

For a second he just stares at me, eyes hard, jaw clenched, and I think he might yell or leave, but then he laughs. He throws back his head and laughs so hard, I think he's going to start crying or pull a muscle.

He has nice teeth, I think absently while he's laughing. I didn't realize how sad and serious he's looked every time I've seen him until I catch this glimpse of rare humor. It's even more attractive than his brooding face.

I'm still standing there, watching him when he finally calms down.

"You're serious?" he asks.

I can't speak anymore. I'm worried that if I open my mouth something else will come out that I haven't foreseen. I nod and look down at my feet.

I don't see his face when he says, "I'm sorry, I just...That's the weirdest thing anyone's ever asked me. I can't do it."

This time, when he steps around me to head to the door, I let him pass.

Chapter Seven

Dispassionate objectivity is itself a passion, for the real and for the truth.

—Abraham Maslow

My interaction with Jensen results in a slew of unfamiliar emotions. I try to identify them in a logical and scientific manner. Shame. Regret. Embarrassment. Maybe a little of all three. I have the inexplicable and intense impulse to cease all attempts at experiencing anything further, but that would defeat the purpose of this whole venture.

It takes me a full night to regain my impartiality and decompress, but by the next day, I'm ready to move on to plan B.

Even though my plans for obtaining experience in the realm of romance seem dubious at best and extinct at worst, I can still examine other types of relationships. Friendship, for one. With that in mind, I call Freya.

"Good morning Lucy," she answers. "You're the only person I know who calls me before eight in the morning. Do you ever sleep?"

"Yes," I answer.

There's silence for a second and I think she must be walking to class because it sounds like she's outside. There's a slight fizz when the breeze hits the phone.

"Everything going okay? I called you last week and you never called me back," she says.

"Yes, thank you, I've been busy. Can you come over tonight?"

"Um, you're going to have to give me more than that, Luce. Am I coming over to study? To field inappropriate questions lobbed in my general direction? To stalk Jensen with night vision goggles and cameras?"

"No," I answer quickly. "My plans regarding my neighbor seem to have been put on hold indefinitely. However, I do wish to discuss possibilities for moving forward. In addition, I wish to pursue a purely platonic relationship with you, and possibly Bethany and Ted in order to enhance my social skills and understanding of various relationships."

"You wanna be my girlfriend, Lucy?" It sounds like she's smiling.

I hesitate for a second. Did she understand my usage of the word platonic? Being that she is a pre-law student at a fairly prestigious university, I will have to assume yes.

"Yes?"

"I thought you'd never ask."

After giving her the address and deciding on a time, I hang up and get to work.

I'm not sure exactly how to prepare for a small, intimate gathering, so after researching a bit online, I decide at minimum I need drinks and food. This makes sense because whenever my brother Sam comes over he immediately raids my fridge. Also, Freya seems to possess an inordinate fondness for food.

After shopping and cleaning up, I'm taking the trash out when I run into Jensen coming up the stairs.

I'm determined to assure him that I'm normal and erase any awkwardness that may be a by-product of our conversation yesterday, so I smile as wide as I can. When he sees me, he stops and looks around. I wonder if he's thinking about running away. Perhaps he's seeking potential witnesses in case I throw myself at him. My face heats at the thoughts. The sensation is foreign. Am I blushing? There are no mirrors around to confirm my suspicion. I don't remember ever blushing before.

I remind myself that the best way to get over an anxiety is to face it head on.

"Hello," I say.

"Hey," he returns.

"I'm sorry about yesterday," I tell him. He's standing at the bottom of the stairs, waiting for me to pass by. I stop on the bottom step so we are nearly eye level and I'm blocking him from going up. "It wasn't my intention to make you feel uncomfortable."

"It's fine, really." He shifts on his feet and looks around again.

I take a deep breath. "I'm having some friends over tonight. If you would like to stop by, you are more than welcome."

"Thanks, that's really nice, but I have plans."

In the bright sunlight of midday, it's apparent that although my initial assessment of his eyes were that they are a plain brown, they're actually dark green. In a stunning burst of clarity, I realize that I think his eyes are pretty. In fact, I think he's pretty. I'm not only intrigued by him, I'm definitely attracted to him. How odd. I hardly know him. Although I suppose a purely physical response is possible and even common. At least, for most people. It's a first for me. But if what Freya said was true about everyone and everything finding him attractive, it's nice to know that in some ways I'm just like everyone else.

"Okay," I say. Putting my internal revelations aside, I step around him and head towards the big green garbage container at the end of the small driveway.

After heaving the bag into the can, I turn around. He's still standing at the bottom of the steps, watching me.

"Are you okay?" I ask.

He jolts a little, as if startled. "Yeah, just fine." Then he disappears up the steps.

***

Right at six, Freya, Ted and Bethany knock on the door. I open the door and they barge in, a whirlwind of laughter and noise. Their hands are full of stuff: a bottle of wine, a twelve-pack of beer, portable iPod speakers, and an orange cylindrical box.

"Drinking Jenga!" Ted announces proudly, holding the box up in the air before putting it on the end of my coffee table.

42

"I don't drink," I say.

"Even better," Bethany says with a crooked grin. "More for us."

"If you pull a drinking block we'll just come up with something else for you to do," Freya says. She walks in and heads straight for the food I have laid out on the counter in between the kitchen and the living room.

"What do you mean?" I ask.

She grins around a mouthful of chips. "You'll see!"

An hour and two rounds of Jenga later I have memorized most of the blocks and their locations. Jenga is a game where you stack rectangular blocks into a tower. Everyone has to pull a block out and place it on the top of the tower without knocking it over. However, the blocks in the game we are playing have different instructions written on each one in various shades of marker. Some of them encourage the player to drink, others instruct the person who pulls it to perform activities such as kiss the person on the left, draw something on the person to your right, remove an article of clothing, and so on and so forth.

We're sitting around my coffee table playing the game, munching on snacks and listening to some rock music Ted put on when the doorbell rings.

"I'll get it!" Freya yells, running to my door. She's the only one who's gotten this far unscathed. Ted is missing his pants but thankfully has boxers on, Bethany has a giant penis drawn on her cheek, courtesy of Ted, and I have a handlebar moustache and beard, courtesy of Freya.

I'm not paying attention to who's at the door. I'm too busy trying to figure out Ted and Bethany's most recent debate. They're trying to decide if it's really better to have loved and lost. I'm afraid I instigated this one, since we started the night off with them attempting to assist me in finding a new direction to take in pursuing the advancement of my emotional education.

"But if you don't know what you're missing, you'll be happily unaware. Ignorance is bliss!" Ted says.

"Then why is it that *everyone* who's never been in love is *always* trying to fall in love. Ignorance is not bliss, ignorance leads to heartbreak," Bethany shoots back.

"Everyone? Always? Really? Our discussions have dissolved into hyperbole? You are cut off that wine, lady!" He reaches for her bottle, and she shrieks and bats his hand away.

"Uh, Lucy?" Freya says from the door.

I turn towards her and at the same time realize that I've been smiling so much that my cheeks hurt. Once I acclimated to the never-ending banter, I began to see the humor in the behavior.

Freya steps aside to reveal Jensen on the other side of the door. My smile fades as my anxiety increases.

I stand and head towards them.

"Hey," he says as I approach. "Someone's parked in my spot."

I say nothing and look at Freya, unsure whose car it is.

"Beth! Move your shit!" she yells into the living room.

"What?" Bethany calls back.

"Your car, doofus, I told you you'd have to move it."

Freya beams a bright smile at Jensen. "Would you like to play Jenga with us?" she asks him sweetly.

"I thought you had plans?" I ask before he can answer.

"I did. They fell through," he says. "Um, yeah, I'd like to join you guys, if that's okay?" He looks at me.

My eyes flick towards Freya. She's standing a bit behind the door so Jensen can't see her and she's nodding emphatically at me and mouthing something I can't figure out.

I move my gaze back to Jensen. "Of course."

Bethany is heading towards us, keys in hand.

I stop her. "I'll move your car. You've been drinking."

"Are you old enough to drive?" she asks.

I frown. "Of course."

"Here ya go." She passes me her keys and then runs back to Ted who's eyeing Jensen up and down unabashedly.

I walk outside and Jensen follows. Freya shuts the door behind us and I hear her squeal through the thin door.

"I'm sorry. I wasn't aware they parked here," I say, walking down the steps with Jensen on my heels.

"No biggie."

"What happened with your other plans?" I ask.

We've reached the bottom of the steps.

"Well." He shifts on his feet and won't meet my eyes.

"I'm sorry," I say when I realize I've made him uncomfortable, yet again. "I don't mean to pry. You don't have to answer that."

"It's okay. I was supposed to meet my dad for dinner but he flaked." He shrugs. "It's not the first time."

"Oh." I'm not sure how to respond to that statement without making him even more uncomfortable, so I walk away.

I hop into Bethany's Jeep and pull out of the driveway, parking it out of the alley and on the street. When I return, Jensen's getting out of his car.

We meet at the bottom of the steps. It's dark outside except for the solitary porch light casting a dim glow on my side of the duplex.

"Nice stash," he says.

"What?"

"Your mustache." He points underneath his own nose.

"Oh, right. I forgot about that."

I step up on the first stair but he stops me with a hand placed gently on my forearm.

"I wanted to apologize," he says.

I turn and look at him. "For what?"

"For yesterday. And earlier today." He removes his hand from my arm, and runs it through his hair. "You caught me by surprise and I haven't exactly been in the best of moods lately."

Now it's my turn to be surprised. Of all the topics I thought he might broach, an apology from him is the last thing I expected. "There's no need to apologize. I'm sure it was inappropriate for me to proposition you the way that I did, and considering I hardly know you. Freya warned me, but I'm not very good at conforming to social conventions."

"I sort of got that," he says. "And don't worry. It was also the best laugh I've had in a long time. Maybe ever."

I smile. "That's good."

"So we're okay?" he asks.

"Yes," I agree.

Once we're inside, I take Jensen's jacket and hang it on the hook next to the door. I move to sit where I was previously next to Ted but he shoves me over and not too gently.

"Honey," he says, handing Jensen a beer while patting the seat next to him. "You sit here."

Jensen smiles. "Okay," he says and sits in between me and Ted.

Ted is positively beaming when we throw in all the blocks and start the game over.

Since Freya is winning—according to Bethany and Ted, and I am not sure how they determined her to be the winner other than she has all her clothes on and nothing on her face— she gets to pull first.

"The first rule of drinking Jenga, is you don't talk about drinking Jenga," Ted tells Jensen while they're rebuilding the tower.

"The second rule is," Bethany starts.

"You don't talk about drinking Jenga?" Jensen supplies.

"Good man!" Ted claps him on the back.

"Also, if you wish to preclude yourself from the activity indicated on the block, the rest of the group decides your punishment," I say.

"Yes! What she says!" Ted nods and lifts his beer in my direction.

Then the tower is ready and Freya pulls a block out of the middle. "Drink to the left," she reads before sitting the block on top of the tower.

"To the left!" Ted says and slugs back his beer since he's sitting on Freya's left.

Bethany's next, she's sitting on Freya's right. "Kiss to the left," she says.

"To the left!" Ted says again lifting his drink in a toast, and we all wait while Bethany kisses Freya on the cheek.

"Prudes!" Ted yells.

"You really want to see that?" Freya asks.

Ted shrugs. "Maybe."

Then it's my turn.

"Take off your clothes and run around the block naked," I read aloud after gently sliding a block from the tower.

I look up at the people around the table who are all watching me expectantly. "It's very cold outside," I say.

"Boooo!" Ted says while Freya and Bethany laugh. Even Jensen gives a low chuckle next to me.

"Also, I could be arrested for indecent exposure." I place the block gently on the top of the tower.

"Oh geez, just take off your shirt and stay in here," Bethany suggests.

That seems like a reasonable alternative. "Okay." I pull my long-sleeved shirt over my head and throw it on the chair behind me.

There's a beat of silence and then Ted gives off a low whistle. "Where is Lucy and what have you done with her?"

"What do you mean?" I ask.

"I mean where have you been hiding that body, girl!"

I'm still a little bit confused about the point he's trying to make. "I haven't been hiding anything," I tell him.

"Oh, leave her alone," Freya tells Ted. She looks at me. "Since you're always dressed like a nun he *incorrectly*," she gives him a pointed look, "assumed you are a prude. He doesn't know you like I do, therefore he doesn't realize that even though you dress like an eighty-year-old woman, you are very scientific and a doctor and probably don't give two hoots about nudity or anything else that the rest of us puritans would think of as risqué."

I nod. "Okay. But I'm not really nude." I gesture to the white bra I'm wearing. It's nothing fancy, plain white cotton. "And I don't really understand modesty. We have no control over the way our bodies are put together, and we are all basically the same."

"Very profound, Spock," Bethany intones.

"Spock doesn't say profound stuff, that's Yoda," Ted tells her.

"Whatever. She's more Spock-like. All logical and stuff."

"True that is," Ted says in a strange, higher pitched yet gravelly voice.

They dissolve into giggles. I'm not entirely sure what they're talking about, but I can't help smiling at their antics and exuberant bursts of laughter.

I turn towards Jensen and see that his gaze is fixated somewhere below my face. "It's your turn."

His eyes fly to mine. "Right."

I'm confronted with his profile while he's pulling his block and I take the time to appreciate his strong jaw. There's a slight flush creeping up his neck.

What does that mean? Is he embarrassed that I caught him staring at my chest? I don't see why. It's a normal male reaction when confronted with a scantily clad female in such close proximity. Even if I were considered grossly overweight or unattractive, he would still be curious, as would any other male in this predicament. Except perhaps Ted.

"Draw something on the person to your left," Jensen reads from the block he pulled.

"Left again? Who made this game?" Ted asks.

"You did," Freya and Bethany say at the same time.

"Draw something on her boob," Bethany suggests.

"No way!" Ted says with an exaggerated grimace. "Her face has been done, though. Draw on her arm," he orders and hands him a black sharpie.

I scoot around to rest my elbow on the table and Jensen takes a drink of his beer before pulling the cap off the marker.

He wraps one hand around my bicep to hold me in place before he presses the marker to my skin. His fingers are slightly chilled—from being outside recently and from holding a cold beer—causing goose bumps to race over my skin.

"Is that okay?" he asks in a low voice. The others aren't paying attention to us. They're talking and laughing, and their voices seem to have melted a little into the background.

"Your fingers are cold."

"Oh, sorry." He pulls his hands back and blows into them, rubbing them together before returning to his drawing position. The marker glides gently over my arm and his hand is now slightly warmer on my bicep.

"You're stronger than you look," Jensen says, gently squeezing my arm.

"I enjoy archery."

"That's an interesting hobby."

"It requires strength and precision."

"And no social interaction. A very solitary pursuit."

I never really thought about it before, but he's correct.

Jensen finishes, pulling away from me and handing the now capped marker back to Ted. I look down at my arm. It's a butterfly, and I'm not sure how he made something so intricate so quickly and with nothing more than a black sharpie. There are accents on the wings as well as swirls around the butterfly, almost making it appear in motion.

"Wow, that's really good," Freya says. Bethany and Freya lean over the table to get a closer look and I hold up my arm for inspection.

"Why a butterfly?" Ted asks.

48

Jensen glances at me before turning back towards him and answering. "I don't know. It just felt right."

Freya is raising her eyebrows at me and Bethany and Ted are throwing each other weird looks, and I'm not really sure what's happening.

"So," Freya says. "Ted's turn!"

Ted pulls his block and reads aloud, "Make sweet, sweet love to a rutabaga."

"Ted!" Bethany and Freya yell at the same time and Beth throws a pillow from my couch at his head.

Later, after we've played a few more rounds and we've all put our clothes back on, Freya is helping me clean up the leftover food in the kitchen.

"Sorry we didn't get around to talking about plan B tonight." She hands me a plate she's just cleaned. I dry it and put it away in the cupboard. I don't have a dishwasher.

Laughter from the living room makes me look over the counter. Bethany and Ted are arguing about something again and making Jensen laugh.

"That's okay. I had fun." I'm surprised to discover I'm speaking the truth. I never have fun around people; I'm usually itching to run away and be alone. But perhaps smaller groups are less overwhelming and the fact we are at my house likely adds to my comfort levels.

"We can get together for lunch later this week and come up with a new plan?" she asks, handing me a cup.

"Yes. That sounds good."

"A plan for what?" Jensen is in the doorway, holding a dirty bowl. Freya takes it from him and dumps it in the sink full of suds.

"A plan for getting her grant back on track since you wussed out on her," Freya answers. She's smiling, but Jensen isn't.

"It's no big deal." I don't want to create any tension.

"Oh. Right," he says. He runs a hand through his hair and an expression of concern flickers over his face so quickly, I wonder if I saw it at all because in the next second he's smiling at us. "Well, thanks for having me over, it was fun."

"You're heading home?" Freya asks.

"Yep."

We exchange goodbyes then he grabs his coat off the rack and heads out the door.

Freya hands me a clean bowl. I dry it and open the cupboard to put it away.

"Seriously, Lucy, what the hell are we going to do now?" she asks.

I can't help but smile. Sure, I have no idea how I'm going to come up with a viable experiment on emotions, but I'm not worrying about it on my own. Just the 'we' in Freya's sentence makes me feel like everything will be okay. Eventually.

Chapter Eight

If you want something, and really work hard, and take advantage of opportunities, and never give up, you will find a way.

−Jane Goodall

"This'll be much easier if you do it my way." Freya is standing in my room, holding a dress that has less fabric than a t-shirt.

"No," I say resolutely.

"Come on!" She shakes it in my direction.

"No."

"Fine. But don't blame me when this doesn't work." She throws the article of clothing onto my bed.

"I don't need to dress like that to get what I want. As a matter of fact, that will send the exact opposite message than the one I'm going for."

"Okay, but for the love of all that's holy, will you please wear something other than a business suit?"

"But this sends the message I want. What I'm offering is a business proposal."

She goes into my closet and comes out with a handful of clothes. "Compromise. This is more than a business proposal. You also need someone you're attracted to and they won't return the sentiment if you look like a woman of strict morals. How about a pair of jeans with a nice top and boots? No slacks, no blazer."

It's a fair settlement. "Fine."

An hour later, we're outside a nightclub. Freya is still grumbling because I didn't let her cover my face in junk. I did make another concession and now the only makeup I have on is a small amount of lip gloss.

She knows the bouncer—a very large, very tattooed bald man dressed all in black—and in less than a few minutes, we're inside the dark cavernous space with the pulsating lights and loud music. It vaguely reminds me of the frat party, but this time at least I have an expert with me. She pulls me around the dance floor to an elevated area that has a variety of couches, chairs and tables. A group of people sit in a circular booth and that's where she leads me.

When we approach, a tall, lanky guy with shaggy, light brown hair stands to greet her.

"Hey, babe," he says, kissing her on the cheek. When he turns his face, I see he has a black eye and his cheek is swollen.

We slide into the booth, Freya first so she can sit next to her friend.

"Lucy, this is Cameron," she introduces him. She has to yell over the loud music.

My eyes fly to her face. "*The* Cameron?"

He laughs. "My girl's been talking about me?" He wraps an arm over her shoulder. Just then, the guy on his right asks him something and he turns his face away from us to answer, giving me a clear shot of the bruising on his face.

Freya leans towards me. "Don't judge me," she whispers.

I'm confused by the statement. "Why would I do that?"

She sighs. "Ted and Bethany aren't here because I didn't tell them about it."

"I thought they had to study."

"Only you would believe that excuse." She shakes her head at me, but she's smiling. "The truth is that Cameron and I got back together, and they don't all exactly get along."

"Why not?"

"Cameron likes to gamble, and he's sort of wild, and the whole cheating on me thing, you know." She shrugs. "He didn't like me hanging out with them so much. He thinks they're judgmental bitches."

I consider her statement and run through my possible responses before answering. My first thought is that Cameron is exhibiting controlling and manipulative behavior. It's common in abusive relationships for the abuser to attempt and

52

isolate the victim from others who care about them, but I don't think this is the proper place for that conversation, and perhaps I am over-analyzing or reading too much into the situation.

"I don't think they would be angry at you," I tell her. "I think they would only be concerned for your well-being."

"I'm sure you're right, I'm just not ready for the lectures, yet."

"Freya?"

"Yeah?"

"What about the, uh, black eye and..." I gesture to the side of my face and then look pointedly at Cameron's injuries.

I very clearly remember our first conversation in the clinic. Freya mentioned, albeit in passing, that there was a person on campus she wished to compensate in exchange for causing physical pain upon Cameron's person. But she didn't actually...?

"Oh, right, that." She bites her lip and avoids my gaze.

"You didn't."

"I sort of did." She leans closer to me, whispering in my ear. "The mob boss guy, I know he's like a thug and stuff, and it was totally wrong for me to hire him to beat up Cameron, but he was kinda hot and I wasn't going to go through with it but then it just happened."

"Freya!"

She groans. "I know, shhh, don't say anything, okay? He doesn't know I had anything to do with it." She gives me a mournful expression. "What was I supposed to do? He had this whole Thor thing going on, and I don't usually find guys with long hair attractive, but..."

I shake my head at her, and before she can continue, the waitress comes over and someone orders a round of drinks. As she's leaving I stop her and order a glass of water.

Once she's gone, Freya leans into me again. "But we're not here to discuss me. We're here for you. Do you see anything you like?" She gestures to the table around us. There's mostly guys, a few girls.

I glance at them, but I feel uncomfortable. This isn't really what I wanted to do, but it's the best option we could come up with for now.

"Well?" she asks when I've been silent for a minute.

"I'm not sure."

My gaze leaves the variety of available guys at our table and moves around the club. From our vantage point, we can see the bar and we overlook the dance floor. It's difficult to make out people on the dance floor because it's mostly dark, but the occasional burst of light reveals faces and bits of the dancers. The bar is better, with lights running underneath the clear surface that exposes the faces of the people crowded around it.

My eyes stop on a guy leaning against the bar and talking to a couple of ladies next to him.

I nudge Freya.

She leans into me. "Yeah?"

"I think I found someone." I point towards the bar. "There, in the white t-shirt."

"With the dark hair?"

"Yes."

She laughs. "You would pick that guy."

"Do you know him?"

Before she can answer, the waitress returns with the shots for everyone. She didn't bring my water and I don't have the opportunity to remind her. A shot is placed in front of me, and I nudge it over to Freya. She takes hers with everyone else at the table and then drinks mine as well.

I can't help but notice that Cameron gives her a slight scowl when he sees her taking the extra shot, but he catches me looking and smiles smoothly.

I nudge Freya with my arm. "You know him?"

"That's Jensen's cousin," she tells me, wiping her mouth with the back of her hand.

"No!"

"Yes!" She's laughing.

"But that's..." I shake my head. "The odds of that are extremely unlikely."

"And yet it's still true. And let me tell you, Jensen is a better choice. His cousin is sort of a douche."

"What does that mean?"

"He's a total player."

"You said Jensen is a total player, too," I remind her. "And my observations indicate otherwise."

"Well, even if Jensen does sleep around, he's nursing a broken heart. He has a good reason to be walking the wild side.

Dominic is, like, a tenth-level douchebag. He's so evil he doesn't have a reflection."

"Well. I find him attractive, and therefore I am going to use him to suit my needs."

She laughs again. "You go girl."

I nod and then scoot to the end of the booth.

"You're going now?" she asks.

"No time like the present. Besides, the waitress didn't bring my water."

"Good luck, be safe and I'll be here if you need anything." She gives me a quick, one-armed hug before I stand and head to the bar.

I maneuver through the crowd so that I end up next to Dominic at the bar. At this distance, I can see he's not as attractive as Jensen, but there is something there. Maybe it's the nose.

I stand there for a minute, waiting to get the attention of the bartender, but he doesn't see me. As a matter of fact, his eyes seem to roam over me whenever he's looking in my general direction, despite my frantic waving.

Finally, when he's close enough to hear me, I yell, "Excuse me!"

He blinks and focuses on me. About time. "Can I please get a glass of water?"

He sighs and looks bored, but complies.

I smile and take my glass. My yelling seems to have garnered some attention. When I turn my focus to the man at the bar next to me, I see he's already looking in my direction.

"You're a bit of a spitfire, aren't you?" Dominic asks.

My smile grows. He sounds like Jensen, that deep gravelly voice. I like that.

"I'm not sure," I answer truthfully. "I wanted water and he was ignoring me."

"That's what you get for not wearing something more revealing." He smiles and nods at my cleavage—or lack thereof—and I start to grasp what Freya meant by douchebag.

"I like it," he continues. "It's refreshing. This place is a total meat-market."

My opinion fluctuates. Maybe Freya is wrong about Dominic like she was wrong about Jensen. He seems honest, at least.

"I'm Lucy." I stick out my hand.

"Dominic," he says. He shakes my hand and holds it a bit longer than is considered appropriate. "What's a nice girl like you doing in a place like this?"

"I'm glad that you asked, actually. I'm conducting research."

"What kind of research?"

"Lucy?" A voice behind me asks. I turn and there's Jensen. "What are you doing?" he asks. His gaze flips to Dominic and then back at me.

"Hey cous! Didn't expect to see you here. I always invite you, but you never actually show." Dominic reaches for Jensen, wrapping his arms around his neck in what might be a hug, but could also be a choke hold. "I thought you were off the market for good, man!" He releases his neck and then rubs his knuckles on his head, a move that Jensen quickly tries to swipe away. "That chick really fucked you up," Dominic says. "This is exactly why I don't do relationships, man. Ninety-nine problems, yanno? What brings you here? Gotta hottie on the line?"

"Right," Jensen says, shrugging out of Dominic's hold. "I came because Freya invited me," he says to me.

"Freya, huh? She hot?" Dominic asks.

Jensen ignores him. "Lucy?"

I know that he wants me to answer his original question.

I shrug. "Plan B?"

His eyes widen, eyebrows lifting, and then he's shaking his head. "No. No. No way. This is not happening."

"What are you guys talking about?" Dominic asks.

Jensen grabs my hand and tugs gently, leading me away from the bar and from Dominic. I suppose I could resist, but I don't really want to.

"I'm sorry!" I call out over my shoulder to Dominic, who looks perplexed. "It was nice meeting you!" And then he disappears behind a wall of people.

"Where are you taking me?" I ask Jensen, but he's not looking at me. He's watching where he's going and the music is too loud for my voice to carry. We weave through the dance floor, around bodies grinding against each other, through the scents of various colognes, sweat and booze, and out the front door into the frigid night.

Once we're a little away from the line of people, he stops and turns, releasing my hand and facing me. "You can't ask Dominic what you asked me. You can't...proposition him."

"Why not?"

"Because he's an ass."

"He's your cousin," I point out.

"I know." He runs a hand through his hair. "Doesn't change anything."

I consider my response before speaking. "All I need is to talk to someone. Ask some personal questions. I don't have much time. I'm wasting time, as we speak. Do you have any other suggestions?"

He stares at me for a beat and the tension between us rises. He can read between the lines. If he can't help me, I'll find someone who will.

"No," he says finally.

"Okay. Thank you for your concern. I'm going back inside." Turning away from him, I head back towards the club.

I make it five steps. "Wait."

"Yes?" I stop, but I don't turn around.

"Okay. I'll do it. Just please, don't ask Dom. He'll totally take advantage of you and then I'll have to kick his ass."

I turn around. "You would do that?" Unbelievable. Someone other than one of my brothers would hurt someone for me. That's new.

"Well, yeah," he says. "I've never," he pauses for a brief moment and his words come haltingly, "met anyone quite like you."

I frown. "Is that good?"

The words themselves sound like it should be a compliment, but the way he said it is questionable.

"I'm not really sure. Look, if we're going to do this, you'll have to work around my schedule." For someone who just agreed to be my mentor, he sure does seem hassled.

"Since my grant has been put on hold, I don't see that as a problem."

"We'll start tomorrow afternoon."

"Okay."

"Now go back in there and find Freya and try not to get yourself into any trouble between now and then."

"I'm never in trouble."

He laughs, but there's not much humor in the sound. "I find that hard to believe. And stay away from Dom."

"I'll do my best." I turn and head back into the club. When I reach the door, I show the bouncer my stamped hand and he lets me back in. I take one last glance behind me and see Jensen turn and head out towards the parking lot, disappearing behind an SUV.

He didn't seem very happy about the arrangement, but as long as my goal is attained and he's willing, I guess it doesn't matter.

Chapter Nine

Words can be sweetly encouraging or downright dirty, but they are almost always a powerful aphrodisiac.

—Dr. Ruth

Jensen didn't indicate precisely what time in the afternoon, so at one o'clock—it is "after" noon, after all—I knock on his door, laptop in hand.

The door swings open, and he's standing there in a t-shirt and jeans. "You're early," he says.

"You weren't specific about what time you wished me to arrive."

He pauses for a second. "You're right. I wasn't."

"Are you available now?"

He glances into his place and then back at me. "Yeah, sure, I guess."

I wait for him to step aside and let me in, but instead he grabs a sweater from somewhere next to the door and then he's shutting his door behind him and yanking the sweater over his head. When he lifts his arms to pull on the garment, I'm given a brief glimpse of defined abdominal muscles. He's not exactly Michelangelo's *David*, but something about seeing the vulnerable swath of skin makes my stomach twist and then drop.

I don't have time to examine that response.

"Can we go to your place?" he asks.

"Okay." What's wrong with his? The fact he never lets me in there makes me want to see it all the more.

He follows me into my side of the duplex and I sit on the loveseat. He sits on the chair to my right. I open my laptop.

"What's that for?" he asks.

"Note-taking."

"Note-taking?"

"I don't want to forget anything and this way you won't have to repeat yourself." I open a blank document. "I'm ready when you are."

He scrubs a hand through his hair and leans forward with his elbows on his knees. "I'm not really sure where to start."

"Why don't you just start at the beginning and we'll go from there."

"The beginning of what?"

"Seduction."

"Seduction?"

I look up at him from my blank screen. "Are you having difficulties comprehending the English language this morning?"

He shakes his head at me with a small smile. "From anyone else, that would be sarcastic, but from you it's sincere. I'm sorry. This is just a little weird. And awkward. I'm not sure how I can teach you this stuff by talking about it."

I know he's right. I'm going to have to experience these things instead of living vicariously through others. I'm just not sure I can broach that topic quite yet. At least, not without sending him running out the door. Again.

"How do you know when you're attracted to someone?" I ask.

"That's...a tough question." He thinks for a second, rubbing his chin with his fingers. I realize he has nice fingers, long and sensitive-looking, but still somehow masculine. He moves them from his chin to his lap. "I guess there's the physical response," he says finally.

I drag my eyes from his fingers to his face. "Do you experience an erection every time you see someone you consider attractive?"

"What?" He looks a bit shocked when his eyes meet mine. "No. I mean, sort of. I mean, not really."

I sigh. "Can you be more specific?"

He thinks for a few seconds. "I suppose if we're talking attraction then I would have to admit that yes, I feel aroused almost every time I see someone I'm attracted to. Or if I think about someone I'm attracted to."

"Okay. That's the scientific response." I really shouldn't have to point out that I am aware of that aspect of it. "I want to know what you feel beyond that."

"Well, there's a difference between finding someone attractive and actually liking someone and wanting to be with them for more than just the carnal part."

"Explain."

"When emotions are involved, everything is just...more."

"More what?"

"More exciting. More nerve-wracking. More intense when it's good, and more painful when it's bad."

I consider this for a moment and try to imagine feeling that way about anyone.

I fail.

"Is this helping you at all?" he asks after a moment of silence.

"I'm not sure."

"You haven't been typing anything."

I look at the blank screen in front of me. "I know."

"So what's next Dr. Lucy?" he asks.

I consider the information he's given me and what I already know about developing relationships. "What about kissing?" I ask. I believe that is the first indicator of an evolving emotional connection. The first milestone, if you will.

"Kissing?"

I raise my eyebrows at him.

"Right. Kissing." He nods and then he's suddenly very focused on me. "Wait, have you ever been kissed?"

"Let's just assume that my experience in that area is negligible," I say.

"Is that a no?"

"It means that my knowledge of kissing is that the exchange of saliva allows lovers to explore the immune system of their partners in order to promote genetic diversity."

His eyes are locked onto mine. His head shakes slowly back and forth. "I can't believe you've never been kissed."

"I've been kissed."

"Then why do you need to know about kissing?"

I shrug. "The kissing I've experienced, there was no passion. It was more clinical, an experiment to see what it might be like."

A small smile plays around his mouth. "Was it with another chick?"

"No."

"Damn."

I frown at him, but his smile only increases from a trifling upward tilt of his lips into a shameless grin.

"If you must know, I kissed a friend—a *boy* friend—I met at science camp when I was sixteen."

"Science camp. That explains why your experience is negligible." He grins at me.

"Now," I say sternly. "Back to kissing."

"Right." He thinks for a moment, pursing his lips and rubbing his chin. "Passionate kissing," he says. "Well kissing is important in that it—" he breaks off and shifts on the chair. "Um, I mean, it leads up to..." Another pause, this time longer. "First you have to—" He stops suddenly and sits up straight. "Listen, I can't do this. If you want to learn about kissing, I'm going to have to show you."

He moves towards me, taking the laptop away and moving it to the table. And then he's right next to me and I don't have time to think about what's about to happen.

"Really, Jensen." I think my heart rate tripled in the last five seconds. "I thought we agreed that you don't want to sleep with me and I have no wish to be a notch on your nearly decimated bedpost."

"Do you want to learn this stuff or not? And my bedpost is intact, thank you very much."

"Well, yes, but—"

"But nothing. Consider this an experiment. And kissing is not sex, not even close. We won't do any more experiments after this. Promise. Unless you beg me. Which you might."

I can't help but smile. "That's a bold statement."

The light is fairly dim in my living room because it's cloudy outside and I don't have any lights on, but he's close enough that I can see the green in his eyes. My gaze is drawn to his mouth. He does have a nice mouth. It's almost perfectly heart-shaped with a plump lower lip. It sounds almost feminine, but when it's combined with his firm jaw and defined cheekbones, and he just looks...kissable. And now that we're talking about it, I can't help but imagine what it might be like.

"You'll show me about...kissing and then we'll discuss the rest of it?" I ask. I find that I'm inexplicably nervous. My palms are sweating, my heart is thumping and I have my hands tightly clasped in my lap because I'm fairly sure they will shake if I try to use them.

"Yes," he says.

"Alright then." I close my eyes and take a deep and slow breath through my nose to try and calm my autonomic nervous system.

A few long seconds later, I'm still sitting there with my eyes closed and I can sense Jensen sitting next to me, but he doesn't seem to be moving.

I open my eyes. "Well?"

He's just sitting there, staring at me. "Sorry," he says. "I got distracted."

I glance around the empty room. "By what?"

"I'm not sure," he says. Before I can close my eyes and prepare myself again, his hands are cupping my face and his lips are on mine.

He's warm and dry and his mouth is soft and gentle. His lips move lightly against mine, a motion that lasts only a few seconds before he's nibbling on my lower lip. That simple, delicate movement ignites something between us. The kiss flashes from simple to explosive and suddenly our mouths are open and I can't get close enough. My hands are in his hair and his hands move from my face to my neck to my shoulders and then under my rib cage, pulling me closer as I'm pulling him closer. Somehow I'm lying down on top of him on the small couch, but our mouths haven't left each other at any point during the transition from sitting to sprawling. We kiss like we're starving and the only sustenance left is each other. It seems to go on forever and yet only for a moment and then I have to come up for air.

When I lift my body up off of his slightly he lets out a small disappointed groan that shoots through my ear drums and straight into my stomach, making my insides throb with something warm and foreign.

I look down at him. His lips are swollen and his pupils are dilated and he's looking at me like he's nowhere near finished sampling my lips. I can feel his body's natural response against my thigh and my body is screaming to let go and follow impulses.

But I've never been ruled by my body. Ever. And I'm not entirely sure what those impulses are, but I am sure that I need to retreat and analyze and contemplate.

"What was that?" I feel a little dazed and fuzzy.

Instead of answering, he tugs me down and we're kissing again and for a second, I lean back into him. It would be so easy to stay here forever. We should be uncomfortable on the small loveseat, but somehow our bodies fit together perfectly, chest to chest, thigh to thigh, legs entangled, hanging halfway off the sofa. But now my brain is waking up and demanding attention. I pull back again after only a few seconds.

"Jensen," I say.

"What?" His deep voice sounds even thicker than normal and it almost makes me let go of what my brain is transmitting.

I sit up, bracing my hands against his chest to push myself into an upright position, ignoring the feel of his chest through his sweater under my fingers. I stand on wobbly legs next to the couch, completely removing my body from his because I believe that's the only way I will be able to have an intelligent conversation. He lies there for a second, takes a deep breath and swallows. I watch his Adam's apple jerk and for a brief flickering moment I wonder what he would taste like there, on his neck, if I were to lean over and lick him.

I shake my head at the primitive thought as if that will remove it from my mind. This is not me. I have control over myself. I have control over my emotions. This is all a by-product of hormones and...and...I don't really know right now, and the lack of knowledge is enough to push me into a state of anxiety.

He stands up, smoothly adjusting himself as he moves and then we stare at each other for a moment.

What does one say in this situation?

"Thank you," I finally manage.

He looks confused for a moment and then he says, "Ahh...you're welcome?"

"That was very enlightening," I say. "What do we do now?" I ask. I'm genuinely curious. This is not something I know how to handle. I've never in my life had such a moment of complete abandon and loss of control.

"I guess, we, um..." He scrubs a hand through his hair and the motion doesn't change the pieces that are sticking up in all directions from when I had my fingers in them. For a second, I'm distracted by the memory.

His eyes meet mine and even though I know it's impossible, I think he can read the thoughts on my face because his eyes widen and I could swear his gaze heats up.

"I'll just see you later," he says. He walks by and stops as if he's going to say something further, but he only pauses for a moment and then he's walking out the door.

I stand in my living room staring at the door for a few minutes, the question I asked still lingering in my mind. What now?

Chapter Ten

I was taught that the way of progress was neither swift nor easy.

−Marie Curie

After my first session with Jensen, I require solitude to figure out how I could lose control of myself so quickly. Even though the sensations I experienced were pleasurable, I'm not sure how I feel about my own overwhelming and reckless behavior and even worse, I'm not sure what to do next.

I also realize after some introspection that when I began this journey, I honestly believed I would never become a slave to lust, like everyone else. I was convinced of my own superiority and that I would be able to control my feelings and observe them in a detached and clinical manner. Now I know that I'm no better and the thoughts shame me. Of course I'm not better. I'm human, and therefore as fallible as anyone.

After a day of analyzing, I haven't come to any conclusions other than confirming my own egocentrism, so I contact my brother Sam for a turn at the shooting range. Out of all of my brothers, he's most like me. He's smart, but in a more artistic way. He's an architect and he's the only one of my brothers who isn't married. In fact, I suspect that Sam is somewhat promiscuous, but that's not a topic I've ever broached with him, and I never will.

"I really don't want to hear about you making out with some dude," Sam says, a counterpoint to my own thoughts about his love life.

I'm standing about ten feet in front of him, positioning my arrow and trying to focus on my stance and the target in front of me, so I can't immediately respond. I accidentally left my own bow at home, something I've never done before. I don't forget anything, ever. The bow I picked out at the range is a bit too tight, but I'm okay with that. It makes me work harder to pull it back before the release. Luckily, the indoor arena is fairly empty in the middle of the day in the middle of the week. There's only one other archer and he's on the opposite side of the large room.

Pointing the arrow at the ground, I place the shaft on the rest and then nock it into place, pulling the bow up and into position, bow arm pointed straight out and my other arm pulled back so my fingers are resting against my face. And again, for the one hundred and third time in the last twenty-four hours, I'm reminded of Jensen and his hands on my face. Right before he kissed me.

I ease the fingers of my drawing hand and the arrow releases, shooting forward and hitting the farthermost ring of the target.

I relax my stance. "I never intended to tell you about making out with anyone." I face him. "You're the one who insisted I tell you what I was thinking. If you can't handle the answer, don't ask."

His response is a laugh. "You're really messed up, huh?" he asks.

I walk over to where he's standing and waiting for his turn. "I am not messed up. I'm just not sure what to do. I don't understand the things I'm feeling. I'm not used to expressing my emotions."

"Yep," he says. "You're messed up. You're not used to *having* emotions, period. But you always know what to do. And you never shoot this badly."

"Okay. Fine." I take a deep breath. "We've established that I'm 'messed up', so are you going to help me or not?"

He's staring at me, not speaking.

"Sam?"

"You like this guy."

"He's nice." I shrug.

"No, you really, really like him. I have to meet him."

"No way." I shake my head. "I barely know him. I like him as much as I like anything I feel a faint fondness for. Like

67

peanut butter. And you can never meet him because you'll do something to make him uncomfortable."

Sam grins. "I know."

Frustrated, I smack him on the shoulder, which is difficult to do with any amount of force because he's over a foot taller than me.

"You're not helping."

"I don't know what to tell you, Luce. It's not like I'm the expert on relationships. You should have asked Tom or Ken, they're the married ones."

"But they're too old and they won't understand. And I'm not in a relationship. I'm trying to experience emotions."

"Well, you seem to be succeeding in that."

"I guess so." I release an exasperated huff. "I didn't think having all these emotions would be so confusing and annoying."

"Welcome to the human experience. What about mom?"

"She doesn't understand me at all. She never has."

"But she loves you."

"I love her too, but we are very different people. She's affectionate and open and I'm..." I trail off and shrug. I don't have to finish my sentence. He knows.

He takes a deep breath and looks at me for a second.

"Okay, Luce. If you like this guy, you have to open up to him a little bit. Relationships aren't easy and it's going to be especially hard for you because you've avoided getting too close to anyone for so long. Or, like, ever."

He walks passed me to the shooting line.

"I told you, it's not a relationship. And I'm close to people."

"I don't count. And neither does mom. Isn't a relationship the whole point of your little experiment?" He quickly finds his stance and nocks his arrow.

I frown.

Sam moves his arrow from aiming position to pointing it at the ground in front of him and faces me again. "You know what? You're not that great about staying close to us, either. When's the last time you called mom?"

"You know I don't like talking on the phone."

"You don't like talking, period."

"Do you have a point?"

"Remember when you were a kid," he begins.

I stifle the urge to groan. Whereas I was born with a lack of verbal expression, my brothers, on the other hand, have the ability to talk and tell stories for hours, like it's nothing.

"Tom and Ken were off at college," he's saying, "and Jon was in high school and way too cool to hang out with either of us. I was nearly a teenager when you were four, so you never had anyone to play with. The other kids on our street always wanted to play sports and get dirty, but you would rather hang out with mom in the kitchen or with dad in the garage. I felt like you were missing out on the typical childhood experience. I would mess with you, do you remember this?"

"Of course. Even if I didn't remember it, you guys talk about it enough at family gatherings that I have it more than ingrained in my memory. You would leave frogs and spiders and other creatures in my bed."

"And what did you do?"

I raise an eyebrow at him, wondering what his point is. "I would analyze them. Involve them in various experiments and then put them back outside. Once, one of the rats died so I embalmed and dissected it."

"You were four."

"And?"

"And you created your own homemade embalming fluid from cleaning supplies and crap you found in the kitchen."

"What does this have to do with emotions and relationships?"

"The point is, if you really want to understand your emotions, it's not going to be easy. You aren't used to being...normal."

"Gee, thanks," I say.

He shoots, finally, and we watch the arrow slam into the target only an inch from direct center.

"Okay. Fine," I say. "What do you recommend that I do?"

He turns towards me. "'Courage is not the absence of fear but rather the judgment that something is more important than fear. The brave may not live forever but the cautious do not live at all.'"

I'm a little surprised at this, it sounds much too poetic for my brother. "That's beautiful, Sam. Who said it, Nelson Mandela?"

"No, Meg Cabot."

I frown, racking my brain. "Who's that? A poet? Philosopher?"

"She writes children's books."

"Oh."

"Listen, Lucy." He walks over and puts a hand on my shoulder. "For once, stop listening to your brain. Follow your gut, your instincts, just let go. What's your gut telling you?"

I look up at him. "I don't know."

He smiles and gives a quick nod. "Good. You know everything. This'll be good for you." With that, he pats me on the shoulder a bit harder than necessary and hands me my bow. "You're up. Try not to suck so much."

***

A few hours later, Sam drops me off in front of the duplex. I give him a quick and clumsy hug before getting out of his large pickup and jumping to the ground.

Halfway up the steps, I notice Jensen standing on the porch just outside his door. He's not alone. An older man is with him, dressed in perfectly fitted slacks and a leather jacket over what appears to be a three-piece suit. He's got lighter hair than Jensen, but the same dark green eyes.

"Hello," I say as I near the top of the steps. They're both staring at me.

"You must be Jensen's neighbor," the man says. "I'm Professor Walker, Jensen's father."

He walks towards me and we meet at the top of the steps. He approaches with a practiced smile and his hand out.

I shake his hand firmly. "Lucy London."

"Ah, yes!" He looks back at Jensen. "You didn't tell me you were living next to our resident genius."

Jensen says nothing. His expression is very serious, and I notice he hasn't shaved and his cheeks are covered in stubble.

"Well, it was nice to finally meet you Lucy." He smiles at me but the smile fades when he turns back to his son. "Jensen, we'll talk soon." And then he's past me and down the steps and gone.

"Are you okay?" I ask Jensen.

His eyes are on me with a sort of focused intensity that makes my insides flutter.

"Yeah."

It doesn't seem that he's going to add anything, so I head towards my door.

"Where were you this morning?" he calls to my retreating back.

I face him. "I went shooting with my brother."

"Was that your brother that just dropped you off?"

"Yes."

Something in his stance relaxes.

"I was thinking." He shoves his hands in his pockets and takes three steps in my direction. "Our interviewing sessions might be more productive if we were more comfortable around each other. If we knew each other a little better. We should...be friends."

I nod. "That makes sense." We've really only been around each other a handful of times. "I need friends," I admit.

"There's an exhibition of new artists at this gallery downtown on Saturday night. I have two tickets."

He doesn't say anything else and I stare at him for a few seconds. "Are you inviting me to go with you?" I finally ask.

He half smiles. "Yeah, I guess I am."

"Okay."

The smile grows. "Okay. I'll pick you up at six."

"Okay." I return his smile and then turn and unlock my door. When I get inside, I'm still smiling.

Chapter Eleven

Life doesn't make any sense without interdependence. We need each other, and the sooner we learn that, the better for us all.
—Erik Erikson

When I update Freya regarding what occurred over the weekend, she lets out a high-pitched squeal so loud that my ears ring and everyone within a fifty-yard radius turns in our direction.

When she stops, I blink at her. "You sound like a rape whistle." The student union hands them out the first week of every semester.

"I'll take that as a compliment," she says.

We're walking through the quad. Freya wanted to go to lunch, but I promised Dr. Heinrich I would help him with his Advanced Molecular Genetics lab. He has a few graduate students who need assistance. Freya agreed to accompany me to the Davidson Science Center.

"He's so into you," she gushes.

Perhaps I shouldn't have told her about my first training session with Jensen.

"I don't think so," I say. "He specifically stated he wants us to be friends."

"Yeah, friends who make out!"

I frown. "Do friends do that?"

"No, idiot!" We walk around a group of guys playing Frisbee. "He's probably going the friend route since you totally freaked out on him after you guys kissed."

"I did not 'freak out'."

"Did you or did you not break contact, and then *thank him*," she says the last two words with disdain, "and then basically force him to leave?"

"I did not coerce him into anything. He left of his own volition."

"So you admit to the first two allegations?"

Despite Freya's frivolous language and playful manner, she may actually be a good lawyer someday.

"Well, yes," I admit.

She gives a satisfied smile. "See? He's making you think you're friends. Lulling you into a false sense of complacency. Before you know it, you'll wake up one morning married with two-point-five kids and his and her BMWs."

"That's not likely."

"Don't like kids?" she asks.

"Don't like BMWs," I say.

"Lucy!" She gasps and stops walking, placing her hand on my arm. "Was that a joke?"

I give her a small smile. "Maybe. I think you're rubbing off on me."

We've reached my building. I stop at the intersection of the sidewalk and face Freya.

"We'll make a normal person outta you yet!" she says. "So, I'll be over on Saturday at five to help you get ready." She's nodding at me with raised eyebrows.

I shake my head. "That's not necessary."

"Yes. It is. It really is. No arguing!" She points at me like I'm a miscreant child and then after a big, goofy grin, she takes off, scurrying down the sidewalk and away before I can formulate a response. I have the sneaking suspicion she's getting to know me pretty well and I'm surprised to discover that I don't hate it.

***

Freya appears in my doorway promptly at 5:00 p.m. on Saturday armed with a bag of goodies and frequent assurances that she's there to make me look classy and not at all "slutted up".

I give in, but only when she shows me the jeans and long sleeve top she's intending on forcing me into.

In the end, I'm fairly satisfied in skinny jeans, boots, a flowing top and colorful scarf. She even has a matching purse. I draw the line at the jewelry.

"But it's sparkly!" she tells me.

"I don't like jewelry."

She shakes her head solemnly. "It's like you're not even human."

"I find it uncomfortable. No matter how long I wear it, I can always feel it. I never lose awareness of something against my skin."

"Freak."

"Yes," I agree.

I kick her out at five thirty. "You need to let me give you a makeover," she says as I'm walking her out the door. "A real one, not this lame just-changing-your-clothes crap."

"I look fine."

She crosses the threshold onto the porch and turns to face me. "You do, you really do, but just imagine a few highlights, maybe a haircut other than straight across the bottom? Your hair is so long and pretty, there's so much you could do with it!"

"Thanks, Freya."

I move to shut the door and she calls out as it's closing, "Don't forget to call me tomorrow! I want details!"

The door clicks shuts.

I go back into the bathroom and wipe off half of the makeup. By the time that's done and I've straightened up my room, it's five forty-five. Fifteen minutes until Jensen said he would "pick me up". But I really don't have anything else to do. I grab the purse Freya loaned me and a jacket and head out the door.

Jensen opens the door in jeans and a button-up shirt, but no shoes.

"I'm ready. I didn't see any point in waiting until six," I say.

"Well, this is a first." He opens the door and steps back to let me in.

"A first what?" I ask. I step past him and inside, glancing around. I'm very interested in his place. He's been so hesitant to let me in during our previous encounters and I can't help but wonder why.

"The first time a girl has had to wait for me to get ready. It's normally the other way around," he says with a smile. "Out in a second." He disappears down the hall.

His side of the duplex is the mirror image of mine, except for a few key details. The fireplace, for one. I had noticed the chimney from the outside before, something that set his side off from mine. Also, my place is rather plain. I don't have much on the walls and all my furniture is functional and mismatched, hand-me-downs from various relatives and garage sales.

Jensen's place is like a model home. His walls are decorated in framed black and white prints. His furniture is all sleek wood and stylish form. He has hardwood floors in the living room and tile and granite in the kitchen.

Everything seems so shiny and new. Except for one thing. There's a side table against a wall, a nice mirror hanging over it. But on top of the side table is an old, squat, white vase. It's not completely white; it's been weathered and slightly yellowed with age. There are a few spots that are nearly brown and there are more than a couple chips on the enamel. It seems such a stark contrast to the rest of the space, I can't help but be drawn to it.

I pick it up and look at it in my hands, turning it around and examining the bottom. There are no distinct markings or signatures on it.

"Do you like it?"

I spin around.

Jensen is leaning his shoulder against the wall in the hallway, watching me.

"It doesn't quite fit." I hold it up and use it to gesture to the rest of the space before placing it down gently where it was.

"That's the point." He pushes away from the wall and steps next to me, running a finger around the imperfect edge of the rim. A breeze of his cologne wafts over me. "It's wabi-sabi," he says.

I tilt my head. "Explain."

He smiles down at me. "Wabi-sabi is a Japanese principle that embodies the idea of transience and imperfection. Like the life cycle. We are born, we get old and we eventually die. Objects are the same, they get old and weathered, but it's not necessarily a bad thing. It's all a part of the cycle of nature. Wabi-sabi is about appreciating the beauty in our naturally imperfect world."

I absorb the words for a minute and appreciate the sentiment.

"It's interesting that this imperfect item is surrounded by perfection," I say.

His smile widens and my gaze is drawn to his lips. Against my will I remember what he tastes like. I force my eyes back to his, but he's no longer looking at me. He's looking down at the vase. I watch him in the mirror.

"My father had this place designed and furbished before I moved in." He picks up the vase. "This was my addition."

"Your rebellion." It makes sense to me now, him not locking his door before he leaves for coffee every Sunday morning. Why should he care about his possessions? They aren't his.

He nods and then puts the vase back down, clearing his throat. "You ready to roll?"

Once outside, he opens the car door for me and I slide across a slightly torn leather seat. I reach over and unlock his side. Since it's an older car, he can't unlock all the doors with a click of a button.

He gets in and turns the ignition, the engine rumbling to life.

There are dents in the dashboard and the carpet at my feet is worn, but it's clean and comfortable.

"Even your car is wabi-sabi."

He smiles at that.

"It's all the original upholstery and interior," he tells me. He tells me more about the car and I watch the lights from the other cars and street play over his face as he talks and drives.

"My dad wanted to buy me something new and flashy, but I had my heart set on a sixty-five Mustang since I was ten. I had to drive to Kansas to pick it up, and I had to log in sixty hours a week of filing and data entry for an entire summer, but it was worth it."

"You bought it yourself?"

"Yep. When I told my dad what I wanted, he refused to give me a single penny. Now I'm glad, though. It's the only thing I've ever owned that's solely mine."

"I've never had a car." I run my hand along the leather armrest on the door.

"Never?"

"I don't need one. I can walk almost everywhere I need to go, and if I'm going to my parents or somewhere else, one of my brothers drives me or I take the bus."

There's silence in the car as he merges into traffic heading downtown.

"How many brothers do you have?" he asks.

"Four."

"Four? That's a pretty big family."

"I suppose so. It feels normal to me. I don't have a point of comparison."

He pulls up outside the art gallery. There's no parking out front and there's a line of people at the door, waiting to get in.

"It's busier than I thought it would be," he says. There's a nervous layer underlining his words.

"Is that a bad thing?" I ask.

"No. I guess not." He shakes his head and then glances at me with a smile. "It's a good thing."

Maybe I imagined his nervousness. Why would he be anxious about an art exhibit?

We drive down the street about a block before we find a place to park.

I get out before he has a chance to open my door, but he holds his arm out for me to take and we walk down the street quickly to get out of the cold.

At the door, a dark-skinned woman with curly brown hair greets Jensen with a giant hug and a kiss on the cheek. "I'm so glad you could be here," she says, holding his hands in hers. "Who did you bring?" She looks at me curiously.

"This is Lucy London," he says, and then to me, "This is Anita Johnson. She owns the gallery."

"It's nice to meet you."

There's no time to exchange further pleasantries; she hands Jensen a pamphlet and we move into the building so that she can greet the people behind us in the line.

The wide open gallery is fairly bustling. Waiters in black and white circle the area with trays of food and drinks. Faint music tinkles through the open space. There aren't many lights shining above us; most of the illumination is reserved for the items hanging on the walls and various standing structures.

Jensen grabs my hand and leads me through the crowd. Much like on campus, he seems to know quite a few people here. We stop a few times while he shakes hands, gets slapped on the back, and makes introductions. I nod and smile and attempt to appear more comfortable than I feel.

Eventually, we make it to the section with oil paintings and I breathe a sigh of relief that I don't have to talk to anyone but Jensen for at least a few moments. I was beginning to feel claustrophobic with all those people pressing in.

"What do you think?" he asks.

I'm thinking that he's still holding my hand, even though it isn't necessary since we aren't moving through people and there's no chance that we will be separated in this less populated area of the gallery, but I realize that's not what he's asking. I look at the canvas in front of us.

"I'm not sure. I presume the artist intended to draw trees in autumn. However, these colors are unlike anything I've seen in nature." Instead of red, orange and yellow foliage, the leaves are a neon yellow, magenta, and the brightest orange I've ever seen. It's almost painful to look at.

"Why do you think that is?"

I consider the question, but there's no logical reason I can ascertain as to why the artist chose this particular palette. "I don't know," I admit finally. "What do you think?"

"I think the artist is in love," he says.

"Why?"

"Because everything seems brighter."

I think about this and shake my head. "That doesn't make sense. Love doesn't affect your photoreceptors." I look the painting over again and add, "I think the artist may have ingested hallucinogens. Scientists have discovered that use of such drugs unlocks the 5-HT2A receptors on the surface of the brain, which in turn affect your other senses, making the world appear and brighter and inaccurate in comparison to reality."

Jensen lets out a short bark of laughter.

"Is that funny?" I ask.

He shakes his head at me. "Every time you open your mouth, you say something I don't expect."

"Is that bad?"

78

"Definitely not. But I win." He pulls out the pamphlet he obtained when we entered and points out the name of this particular piece. It's entitled *Falling in Love*.

"Get it, *falling*?" he says, nudging me with his elbow and giving me a crooked smile.

"I'm not sure if that's clever or ridiculous. And you're not allowed to use the title of the piece in your assessment, that's cheating," I say, but I find that I'm smiling.

I have to presume he enjoys my commentary and lack of artistic intelligence because he pulls me around to a few other sculptures and paintings, and he asks me a variety of questions about each one, mostly laughing at my responses.

"I'm afraid I'm not very good at analyzing art," I tell him when we're sitting on a narrow bench together eating a few appetizers on small plates in our laps.

"I think you're great at it. So great in fact, that you may have missed your calling as an art reviewer." He eats a small bite of chicken satay off a toothpick.

"Perhaps," I say. "I have no idea what my calling is. Art critic is just as likely as court jester at this point." Homeless person might be my job description if I don't figure out an experiment in emotional pathogens.

He finishes swallowing his food before meeting my eyes and responding. "I think you're selling yourself short. I have no doubt you are capable of anything you set your mind to."

I watch his unwavering gaze. It's a nice feeling, someone I'm not related to having so much faith in me, however misguided and inaccurate it might be.

I smile at him and pop a bacon-wrapped scallion in my mouth.

"There you are!" Anita, the gallery owner, appears next to us and lays a hand on Jensen's shoulder. "Are you guys enjoying the exhibits?"

We smile and nod.

"Do you mind if I steal Jensen away for a minute?" she asks me.

I shake my head no while still chewing a mouthful of food. I finally swallow. "Of course not."

"Feel free to look around and enjoy the appetizers and drinks," she tells me with a smile. She pulls him away and to the other side of the gallery where they disappear through a door marked private.

I wonder what that's all about. I finish the remaining bite of food left and throw the plate in a sleek silver trash in the corner. I pick up the pamphlet Jensen left on the bench and weave through the people still milling about.

There's only one more section of the gallery I haven't seen. We walked through the first two—the oil paintings and the sculptures—each separated by a low wall.

The third and final emerging artist on display features all charcoal drawings of people. But not models. At least, not in the sense of the word that implies tall, thin and perfect.

There's an old man with a double chin, a small child with a cleft pallet, and the profiled form of a beautiful woman with a missing leg. The drawings themselves are fairly simple, at least at first glance, but I realize there are all kinds of details only apparent upon closer inspection. The glimmer in the old man's eyes, the dimple in the child's cheek.

It reminds me of wabi-sabi, finding beauty in imperfections. Jensen knows the gallery owner, maybe he knows this artist as well and that's where he learned the concept.

I read through the leaflet. All of the other works have the name of the artist along with the title of the drawing, but these just have the titles. And the titles themselves are fairly generic: man, child, woman.

"What do you think of this one?"

I don't bother turning to face him because I would recognize his voice anywhere, that deep, gravelly pitch. He's standing next to me, his shoulder brushing mine.

"It's different from the others," I say.

"Different good or different bad?"

"Definitely good. But I'm not sure exactly how to describe why. It's less...pretentious."

He laughs, a deep resonant chuckle that makes goose bumps rise over my arms.

"Are you hungry?" he asks.

"Yes." I missed lunch and the few bites of appetizer didn't do much to assuage my hunger.

"Let's get outta here." He grabs my hand and we twist back through the crowd.

We pick up a pizza on the way back to the duplex and end up at his place, eating at the granite bar between the kitchen and the living room.

"So, tell me more about your brothers and the rest of your family," he says. I'm sitting on a bar stool at the counter and he's in the kitchen across from me, opening cupboards and retrieving plates and napkins. He slides a plate down the counter to me and I catch it. I pop the lid on the pizza and dig in.

"There's not much to tell," I say, putting three pieces of pizza on my plate. "My brothers are all much older. Sam is the closest to me in age, he's about eight years my senior. Tom is the oldest, then Ken and Jon. Sam is about twelve years younger than Jon."

"That's quite an age difference." He stays on his side of the counter, pulling his own slices onto his plate.

"I was a surprise. My mother had me when she was in her forties. She was happy to finally have a girl." I take a bite of the pizza.

"I bet they were even more excited to have a genius child."

I shrug. "I don't think so."

"What do you mean?"

"They didn't really know what to do with me."

"But still, they must be really proud of you."

I just nod because I'm not sure. They've never communicated that to me and I've never asked.

"How long have you lived here?"

"For the last two years, since I was eighteen. Before that, I would take the bus here every day."

"Your parents boot you out at eighteen?" he asks with a smile.

"No. My parents didn't want me to move out, but I wanted to. I love my family, but I don't enjoy living with other people."

"Why not?"

I consider his question before answering. "Being alone is easier."

"Easier? Or more controllable?"

I pause again. "Both." I'm not entirely sure what else to add. I feel slightly unnerved that Jensen seems to understand me better than I understand myself and we hardly know each other.

We munch on pizza for a little bit and in between bites I ask, "What about you?"

"What about me?"

"Do you have any brothers or sisters?"

"Nope. Only child. Just one creepy cousin."

"He's not creepy."

"You don't know him well enough." He smiles.

"What about your father?" I can't help but ask. I've wanted to know ever since their exchange last week and if it's appropriate for him to ask about my family, I have to assume the reverse is also true.

"What about him?"

"You don't get along."

Jensen sort of nods and shrugs at the same time, pulling another slice from the box and picking at the toppings. "We don't always agree."

He doesn't seem inclined to expand so I stay quiet and hope the thoughts rolling around in his brain will eventually spill out of his mouth.

"When did you move out?" I ask when it doesn't seem he's going to elaborate.

"Same as you. Eighteen. I lived in the dorms until last semester when this place opened up."

"Did you like the dorms?"

He grimaces. "Not really. Have you ever shared a bathroom with three dudes?"

"No, my two eldest brothers had moved out by the time I was able to use the bathroom."

He shakes his head. "It's not pretty."

I look down at my plate and realize I've finished my pizza. I stand up to put my dirty dish in the sink, but when I move around the counter into the kitchen, he stops me.

"I didn't always want to be a lawyer," he says finally, taking my dirty plate away and placing it on top of his, walking both of them to the sink. He turns the faucet on, splashing water over our dirty dishes.

I'm not sure if he's changing the subject or not.

"What did you want to be?" I ask.

"Anything that my dad wasn't. Anything that he didn't approve of."

"Why?"

"He's not always a nice person," he says.

"No one is always a nice person," I say.

That makes him smile, a little. "That's true, but my dad can be a real prick."

I tilt my head at him. "Explain."

82

"Where do I start?" He gives a short laugh and shuts off the tap, turning his body to face me and leaning back against the counter. He crosses his arms over his chest. "You're probably going to think it's stupid, and it probably is. I'm just a poor little rich boy with First World problems."

"You're not being fair to yourself. The amount of wealth your family has doesn't make your feelings less valid than anyone else."

"Maybe you're right." He watches me for a second and then looks away. "Our most current debate is over my future. I've decided I'm going to pursue civil rights law."

"And your father doesn't approve?"

He shrugs. "He wanted me to go into corporate law, like him, but he'll accept it. Eventually. For him it's better than the alternative."

"What's the alternative?"

He opens his mouth to speak, but then stops and shakes his head. "Anything. It doesn't matter what I want to do, I do what he tells me. Mostly."

I think carefully before I speak. I know how I want to respond, but I also don't want to offend him or make things awkward. I think a little about what Duncan told me, and how I had made mistakes in the past while counseling others.

"You don't have to let anyone else dictate your life," I say finally. "They aren't the ones who have to live it. You give your father more power than he has."

He shakes his head. "You don't understand."

"You're right, I don't. I've never had to deal with overbearing parents. If anything, by the time I came around, my parents were too compliant. But if you're not happy with the path your father is forcing you down, you're the only one who can change it."

There's silence for a moment and I wonder how he's going to respond. He can't complain to Duncan, but he can avoid me and for a fleeting second I think that might be worse.

"Logically, I know you're right," he says. "But the saying and the doing are two entirely different things."

"Fair enough," I concede. "I understand that sentiment completely."

"So tell me," he says. He walks past me to the living room.

I follow him to the couch and sit on the opposite side, leaving a good two feet between us.

"If you have such a large family," he asks, "why is it that you have to go through this whole socialization experiment?"

A very neat maneuver to remove the conversation from him and turn it back to me. I smile at him to let him know I'm onto him. "Since my brothers are significantly older than me, by the time I came along, they were all too old to play with, and I was never much for behaving like normal children."

"Oh, yeah? What kind of stuff did you do?"

I shrug. "Mostly taking various objects apart and then attempting to put them back together."

He looks intrigued. "Like what?"

"It started with small things like clocks, watches, things like that. Then I moved on to the dryer, dishwasher, and fridge. I spoiled a whole week's worth of food once, playing with the fridge."

He laughs. "So while other little girls were playing with dolls and games, you were playing with household appliances."

"More or less."

"That's pretty amazing."

"Or odd."

"Nah, never that," he says. "Well, I'll admit when we first met I did think you were pretty odd. But now." He stops and shakes his head. "Now I appreciate your bluntness. Trust me, when you've been lied to by the people you're closest to, you start to place a high value on honesty."

He's still smiling and our eyes meet and we stare at each other until I start to feel strange and uncomfortable twinges somewhere in the vicinity of my heart.

His eyes are dark in the muted light and I experience a sudden and compelling desire to lean in closer and press my lips against his. To feel the loss of control again, just for a minute. The same loss of control that had me confused and reeling before. Why would I want to do that again?

"I have to go," I say instead. And then I'm standing and grabbing my jacket and heading for the door with Jensen close on my heels.

"Are you sure? I can make some coffee or—"

"No. That's fine. Thank you for a very nice evening," I say quickly and then I'm out the door and across the porch.

When I get my door open, Jensen calls out behind me from his open doorway. "Good night, Lucy."

I don't turn around. Instead I call back, "Good night," and then I shut the door firmly behind me. I shut it on Jensen, but I can't shut it on myself and on the strange and foreign feelings churning inside.

Chapter Twelve

The best scientist is open to experience and begins with romance – the idea that anything is possible.

–Ray Bradbury

On Thursday, I stop at the clinic and check in with Duncan. I tell him about my new friends and some of the things I've done over the last few weeks.

I also open up to him about what's happening with Jensen, and my own confusing reactions.

"Why do you think it is that when you start feeling something you've never felt before, you want to run away?"

"I don't know."

"How many times have you said, 'I don't know' in your life?"

I rifle through my memory banks. "A handful of times, approximately."

"And of those times, how many have been since I last saw you?"

"Most of them."

"For someone who always knows everything, or knows how to find the answer, not having the answer might be scary."

I consider his words in relation to the sensations I've been experiencing over the last two weeks. I blink at him. "I'm scared of my own feelings."

Every time I've felt something I don't understand, I've either pushed or ran. And I've been doing that because I don't like how someone can affect my emotions without my consent.

"It's not logical to be afraid of myself." I shake my head and try to think it through. "I've always been able to control how I feel. Most people allow external sources outside their control affect their emotions, and I've always prided myself on being more logical."

"'Harsh words or foul blows are not an outrage in themselves, but your judgment that they are so'," Duncan quotes.

I nod. "Epictetus."

He smiles. "If you care about someone, it's okay for them to affect you, as long as you are aware, and they aren't willfully trying to hurt you. The more you open up to people, the more emotions you will experience because you're going to care about them and about how they perceive you."

"I do care."

There's something about his words that resonates with me. Caring about someone means allowing them to affect your emotions. Handing over some control to them. It's terrifying, and thrilling all at once. I wonder if there's a way to test that. Are you more likely to experience the effects of someone else's emotions if you care for the person being subjected to them?

"That's really great, Lucy," he says, cutting off my train of thoughts.

I mull over everything we've revealed, and Duncan sits in silence while I think. He always knows when to speak and when to let me absorb.

"So I can come back and start working on my project again?" I ask.

He leans back in his chair. "Do you have a viable hypothesis?"

"Not yet. But I will, soon." I feel frustrated. I have goals. I have things I want to learn and this is getting in the way.

"Lucy, you have another month. The board agreed to wait and give you the extension because they trust you will figure it out. Use this time. Stop stressing. You're young. Just live. Have fun. Forget about school for a bit. You've spent your whole life working and studying. It's time to focus on you. Everything else will fall into place."

I leave the clinic and head home, thinking about what Duncan said.

Every time I've seen Jensen since last weekend, my heart rate picks up, adrenaline surges into my system. It's as if my body is experiencing a fight-or-flight response, but there is no threat. Except for the threat of another kiss. Not that I didn't enjoy the kiss; it was more that I enjoyed it too much. When I'm with Jensen, it's as if everything disappears. Except him. And me.

Maybe it's too much. Maybe I can't handle it. Maybe I should find someone else to interview. No, the thought makes me panic even more. There is no one else. What I should be doing, what any good scientist would do, is take Duncan's advice and figure out how to get the most out of the time I have left.

I hear voices as I approach the duplex along with the now familiar rumbling sound of Jensen's laugh.

Freya is outside my door and Jensen is sitting on the railing, his back to me, talking to her. He says something and she laughs, flicking her brown hair over one shoulder and putting her hand on Jensen's arm.

I stop at the bottom of the steps and something dark flows through my mind. I have the sudden and disturbing image of forcibly removing her hand from him and tossing her over the side of the railing.

"Hey," I say, walking up the steps.

What is wrong with me? Am I sick? I would never do that to Freya. Why would my brain offer such an image for consideration?

"Hey girl! I was waiting for you. Did you forget we have a date?" she calls out.

"We do?" I ask when I reach the porch. I'm relieved to see that Jensen is now upright and has moved at least two feet away from Freya. I shudder to think what distressing thoughts might run through my head if they were any closer or, heaven forbid, touching again.

She grins at me and throws an enthusiastic arm around my shoulder, and I feel horribly guilty all over again. "I'm taking you to one of the best places to observe human behavior at its most basic level."

"Okay."

"Are you ready to go now or do you need anything?" She gestures to my door.

"No, I'm good."

We say goodbye to Jensen and then head to Freya's car, parked down at the end of the alley.

She drives an old, beat-up VW bug and I have to crawl through the driver's side to get to the passenger seat.

"Sorry," she says, grinding the stick shift into place and lurching down the street. "I haven't had money to get the door fixed. And my mom's all like, 'you've got to learn to be responsible and the value of the dollar and blah, blah, blah,'" she mimics using her fingers for air quotes, which makes me nervous since she removes her hands from the wheel.

Just in time, she puts her hands back on the steering wheel to make a left-hand turn, without looking either way, and nearly collides with another vehicle. I grip the handhold on the door as the other driver honks and yells something colorful out the window. Freya waves and smiles in his direction.

I'm scared to ask why the passenger side door is broken.

"Where are we going?" I ask, hoping it's somewhere close.

"You'll see. You are gonna love this," she says.

I have a feeling I'm going to regret this, actually, but I manage to remain calm as she careens around a few more turns before stopping and parking in a giant parking lot next to a sprawling building.

"The mall," I say, glancing out the window at the behemoth structure.

"This is where youth go to test out their relationship-building skills," she says, giving me an excited smile. "You'll see."

She leads me into the building, and we go straight to the food court. Since I'm with Freya, I'm not really surprised this has to do with food. But she's right, there's a ton of pre-teens and older teens, all milling about. Flirting, messing with each other. I could probably sit here and watch for hours.

"Told ya." She smacks me gently on the arm. "This is where a lot of them come after school gets out. Now let's eat. I'm starving!"

We order some Chinese and find an empty table. As we consume questionable cuisine she tells me about her latest drama with Cameron. It seems he's been ignoring her texts and not returning her calls and she heard through a mutual friend that he was seeing someone else. I find that I'm relieved.

"Are you really surprised?" I ask her.

"I guess not, I just thought, you know, that he changed. That I could change him. Isn't that stupid?"

"It's not stupid," I tell her. "He should be able to stay monogamous for you. You're worth it."

"It's because I wouldn't sleep with him again," she says taking a bite of sweet and sour chicken and chewing it up before continuing. "When we got back together, I told him I wanted to wait, that I had to be able to trust him again before we took that step." She sighs and shoves an egg roll in her mouth and chews it slowly.

"You should never compromise your morals for someone else," I tell her. "You did the right thing. Except for the part where you had someone beat him up. That's probably not the right thing."

"I know," she says with a laugh. "Thank god he never found out. Thanks, Luce. You're a good friend." She pats my hand and we dig into our food.

Freya is halfway through her general's chicken, and I've only taken three bites, when I can't keep it in any longer.

"I have to talk to you about something," I say.

She chews and swallows. "Yeah?"

"It's about Jensen."

She smiles and takes another large bite. "I'm not surprised, are you guys lovers yet?"

"What? No, it's not that. Not even close." I take a fortifying drink of water and look straight at her. "When I came home today and saw you talking with him, I felt...angry."

She stares at me for a few long seconds. "Is that it?"

"Is that it?" I repeat. "No, that's not it. I imagined something awful."

She leans forward, eyes gleaming, smile widening. "Do tell."

I sigh in frustration. She's smiling now, but she's going to hate me. "I imagined ripping your arm from him, and tossing you over the balcony!" I cover my mouth as soon as the words leave it, ashamed and yes, embarrassed. I recognize these emotions immediately as well as the heat creeping up my neck.

I watch her expression, expecting her to be upset with me, but she bursts into laughter.

"Why is this funny?" I ask, alarmed at her response.

"You like him."

"Well, yes he's nice."

"No, you like him. Like, really like him. Would you quit denying it? It's totally obvious to everyone but you."

I sigh. "You sound like my brother. Yes, he's a kind person and I enjoy being in his presence. I also happen to find him attractive. That's it."

She laughs. "What do you think that means? Oh, it explains everything. You want to be his girlfriend. You want to marry him and have a million of his babies."

"No." I shake my head in denial and stare down at my plate like it holds the answers.

"Yes."

"No!"

"Well, Ms. Scientist, what do you think of the fact that you're jealous when other females talk to him?"

"Jealousy in its most basic form is the fear of losing something to someone else," I say.

"You think I'm going to steal Jensen from you," she teases.

I'm confused. "He's not mine to lose," I insist. "These emotions aren't logical."

"That doesn't matter when you like someone. You found him attractive and then you talked to him and he's not a total creepazoid. You like him. It's okay, you can admit it. Nothing to be ashamed of. I won't judge you. Honestly, I would judge you if you didn't feel anything for him. And it's okay if you want to throw me off your porch, as long as you don't actually do it. Not that you could. I could totally take you down even though you've got like seven inches on me. I'm tenacious." She laughs and shakes her head. "I can't believe you told me that, though." She chuckles softly and then stuffs the last few bites from her plate into her mouth.

I examine for the millionth time the emotions that have been coursing through my system whenever Jensen is around. Anxiety, lust, happiness...the fact that he has an effect on my emotions that I can't stop or control. Oh god.

"I do like him," I say. "I think I like him a lot." How horrifying. "What do I do?"

"What do you want to do? Do you want to pursue something with him? A relationship?"

"I have no idea. How do I find out? And is it even possible? I don't think he feels the same for me. And even if he did, I'm not sure I could handle a relationship. I'm not good with all the talking and being around people all the time."

She makes a derisive noise. "I think it's more than possible, and I think you're better with people than you realize."

"I don't know, I mean, look at him and look at me. We're so different. And he's..." I don't know how to describe it. "He's handsome and charming and socially stable. I'm..."

"Honey, you're a hottie in horrible clothing."

"No."

"Yes. Those lips, those eyelashes that have never seen mascara, that skin, that body."

"No."

"Dude, get rid of the orthopedic shoes and corduroys and you are a knockout."

"I've never understood the compulsion to restrain one's feet in an apparatus designed to invoke pain and potentially damage the nervous system."

"Plus you're funny!"

I frown.

"Maybe not intentionally funny." She pushes her plate aside, and leans towards me. "Let me fix you up. Please? It's all I want for Christmas," she begs.

"I've let you dress me before and it's not even Thanksgiving yet." Although the holiday is quickly approaching. "I don't have enough money for a new wardrobe, nor do I need one."

"I have friends who work here. They can help."

"I don't know."

"I know," she says. "Trust me."

I can feel my resolve wavering.

"I don't want to seem desperate." I don't really care how I seem, and surely she knows this, but I'm running out of excuses.

"Blame it on me."

"You're relentless."

"So I've been told."

I stand up and grab my tray. "Fine. But nothing too dramatic."

92

She screeches like a banshee and jumps up and gives me a hug.

"This is going to be so much fun!"

Three hours later I've been primped, prodded and shoved into designer labels. Freya knows everyone. She has a friend at the salon in the mall who gives me a trim and styles my hair for free. I draw the line at any kind of chemicals in my hair though, so that goes pretty quickly.

Next, she takes me to a friend of hers named Jenny who's a personal shopper at a major department store. Jenny bustles us into the back, behind closed doors where they keep items that are going to be sold or donated due to minor defects such as missing labels, uneven stitching and small tears in the fabric. She leaves us there to go through the giant piles and it takes over an hour of sorting through sizes and styles until Freya is happy with a variety of boots, sweaters and pants for herself and for me.

"Wasn't that great?" she asks as she's driving us out of the mall parking lot.

"Yes." I'm afraid to elaborate or argue because if she starts talking, that means she's not fully concentrating on the road and I'm convinced we won't survive the trip home.

"Okay, now we need a plan to get Jensen's attention and see if he likes you as much as you like him," she says.

"I'm sure my transformation into fashion icon Barbie will be more than sufficient."

"Oh, please." She narrowly misses hitting a trash can on the curb as she's rounding a corner. "You barely look any different. I think you have a distorted view of yourself. I mean really get his attention, like how when I was flirting with him got your attention."

"How are we going to accomplish that?" I cringe as she rolls through a stop sign.

"By making him jealous, of course."

Chapter Thirteen

Only two things are infinite, the universe and human stupidity, and I'm not sure about the former.

—Albert Einstein

"I don't think this is such a great idea, Freya."

We're sitting in my living room, waiting for my fake date to arrive.

"Of course it's a good idea! Maybe he likes you, but he doesn't know that he likes you. If he sees you with someone else, he'll realize that he's jealous, and that he's always loved you and he'll burst in here, all bulging biceps and unspent fervor, and he'll challenge Tony to a duel and you'll fall passionately into his arms, his lips crashing down on yours..." Her eyes have glazed over, and she's not even looking at me anymore.

"Freya?"

"Hmmm?" She's still gazing off into the distance, at a daydream only she can see.

I snap my fingers in front of her face and she startles a bit before meeting my eyes.

"What if he decides I must not like him and he gives up? And this is all assuming he has the smallest inkling of feelings towards me. He might view me as a sister or mere friend, in which case all your efforts will be for naught."

"What? No way. Who knows more about relationships and snagging a guy, me or you?"

94

I raise an eyebrow in her direction. "I'm not entirely sure considering you've recently lost your virginity, and your boyfriend cheated on you and then you had him beat up before you took him back, and now he won't call you."

"Forget all that." She waves her hand dismissively. "Trust me on this, okay?"

I sigh. "Okay."

Her friend Tony comes over, and he's so obviously gay that I start to relax. Jensen will immediately realize that I'm not dating him.

When the rumble of Jensen's Mustang sounds in the driveway, Freya shoves us out the door. Tony takes my hand and gives me a brilliant smile. He's really good-looking, in an almost feminine way. He's tall and thin, but leanly muscular with angular features and clear blue eyes that stand out of his darker complexion. He's very well dressed and clean shaven, and his dark hair is styled in that perfectly tousled way.

He pulls me down the steps as Jensen is coming up them. I try to remove my hand from Tony's, but he just holds on tighter.

"Hey," he says to Jensen.

"Hey," Jensen returns. His gaze roams over us and pauses on our linked hands, and I silently will Tony with my mind to say something else to reveal that he prefers people with Jensen's reproductive organs over mine.

We're stopped on the steps and they're both staring at me and I have no choice but to make introductions.

"Jensen, this is Tony. Tony, this is my neighbor Jensen."

"How's it going man?" Tony extends his hand that's not linked with mine and surely the shock that's pulsing through my body is revealed on my face.

All of a sudden Tony sounds completely not gay and totally masculine. He shakes Jensen's hand and I can tell he does it firmly and confidently, and then Tony turns to me and says, "Are you ready, babe?" and I cannot reconcile the creature in front of me with the same man that burst into my house and squealed like a little girl only a half hour ago.

"Yes," I manage to squeak out, and then he's pulling me down the steps. I throw a look over my shoulder and see Jensen still standing on the steps, watching us. I can't see his eyes or his expression clearly. All I know is I feel that I've done something terribly wrong.

When we are out of sight, Tony drops my hand.

"So, what did you think?" he asks excitedly.

"I can't believe you do that so well," I say, amazed.

"Oh, you are too sweet, honey. Didn't Freya tell you I'm a theater major?"

"No, she didn't."

"You should have seen the look on your face!" He claps his hands together. "Now, hurry up doll, let's go get some stuff to make martinis and we can celebrate!" He shimmies his shoulders.

***

Three days later, I've confirmed what I suspected all along. Trying to make Jensen jealous was a bad idea, and it's backfired in the worst possible way.

"She's back," I call Freya one afternoon.

"What? Who's back?"

"The leggy blonde."

"What the heck are you talking about? And why are you calling me now and not at seven o'clock in the morning? My whole world view is shattered."

"Remember when I was observing Jensen in order to ascertain his habits?"

"Never repeat that to anyone but me. You sound like a crazy stalker. And yes, I remember."

"There was a blonde who came over a few times. She stayed for a few hours and left. She hasn't been there since...well, since before Jensen and I, *you know*, but now she's back. I just saw her go into his place."

"She stays for a few hours and leaves? Do you think she's a hooker?"

"What? No! I mean, I don't know. He hasn't talked to me since he saw me with Tony. I haven't really seen him around. He's avoided all communication with me, and now this!"

"I can hear your hands wringing from here, Lucy. Listen to me. It's going to be okay. Calm down, I'll be there in twenty minutes."

She hangs up on me before I can say anything else.

I pace back and forth in my small living room. What do I do now? What do normal people do?

My gaze falls on the iPod and speakers that Tom left the last time he was here.

Twenty-five minutes later, there's a knock and then Freya lets herself in. She stops in the entryway and stares at me with her mouth open.

I'm on the floor in my PJs with an open pint of ice cream in front of me.

"Are you listening to Taylor Swift?" she asks.

"I get it now!" I wave my spoon at her. "I knew he was trouble when I walked in."

"When he walked in," she corrects.

"Right, and the story of us *does* look a lot like a tragedy now!"

"Oh, Jesus." She kicks the door shut behind her with her foot because her arms are full of groceries.

"If I could play the guitar, there would be teardrops on it." I take a bite of Chunky Monkey and consider that statement. "If I ever cried," I add. "Which really only happens when I cut onions due to the propanethiol S-oxide."

"I've created a monster," she moans.

"You know, junk food really does make me feel better. At least temporarily. I suppose it's the increased chocolate intake triggering a dopamine release."

"Well, then you're in luck and we'll really be working out those dopamine receptors because I brought more." She walks to the kitchen and puts her bags on the counter.

"Have you ever seen *Bridget Jones' Diary*?" She holds up a DVD and waves it at me.

Two hours later, she's lying on her stomach across my small sofa and I'm on the ground near her feet with my back resting against the bottom of the couch while we watch Bridget kiss Mr. Darcy in the snow in her underpants.

"I'm sorry about that whole thing with Tony," Freya says.

I try to hand her the bowl of popcorn but she waves it away so I put it on the coffee table.

"That's okay. I think we made a serious error in judgment. Jensen is still recovering from the loss of his long-time girlfriend to his best friend. He likely has trust issues and now I've exacerbated them, assuming he felt any small inkling of anything for me beyond friendship. Besides, this is what I needed after all, to experience emotions universal to people in my age group. And really, it's not so bad."

"That's the pound of chocolate cake talking," she says.

I consider that. "Maybe."

She sits up and puts the remote on the table next to me. "You're lucky. The whole thing with Jensen ended before it got too serious. The longer the relationship, the more it sucks when it ends."

"That makes sense. Are you okay? About the whole Cameron thing?"

"You know, for a while I didn't think I would be. But now...I'm glad. You were right, I deserve better."

"Good. Did you ever tell Bethany and Ted about Cameron?"

"Nope. I love them, I really do, but." She wrinkles her nose, "They're too honest sometimes. Sometimes I need that, and sometimes I need no questions asked. With Cameron, I already know I made a huge mistake; I don't need anyone reminding me."

She leans forward and gives me a half hug. "This is why I love you," she says. "You are so non-judgmental. And you're not competitive or jealous. So many girls are like that, in an underhanded and sneaky way."

"It's not really their fault," I tell her. "A lot of females in our society are naturally competitive but they are forced to suppress those inclinations due to socioeconomic and cultural factors beyond their control."

"See? You even make excuses for the bitches."

I stand up and start picking up our trash. "Did you want any more frosting?" The tub is half empty and I wave it at her.

"Nah." She stands next to me and grabs a few pieces of trash and napkins off the table and we take everything to the kitchen.

"What are you doing for Thanksgiving?" she asks.

"I'm going to my parents' house for the day. They live in the highlands. You?" I put the frosting in the fridge.

"I'm going home for the week, leaving Monday. Hopefully it won't snow and delay the flights. I heard there might be a storm coming in next week." She tosses everything into my trash and we head back to the living room.

"It's snowing now." My pale white curtains don't hide the outside world to a large degree, and I can see a few flakes

98

flickering down in the street light. "You could stay here tonight. This is a sofa bed." I thump the cushion with my hand.

Her eyes widen. "You wanna have a sleepover?"

"If that means you stay the night here, then...yes?"

She squeals. "Yes! I haven't done that in years! Come on." She grabs my hand and pulls me down the hall towards the bedrooms.

"What are you doing?"

"If this is your first sleepover, we're going to do it right."

A couple hours later, my hair is done in about twenty different braids of various thickness, and pinned back in multiple ways to make them form different sizes of circles around my head. My nails are painted and I'm attempting to do Freya's toes. She's sitting on the couch with her feet in my lap.

"Isn't this fun? It's better to have sleepovers when you're older. When you're young, you run the risk of your friends putting your panties in the freezer, or the old hand in a water cup trick."

I finish her toes and glance at the clock. It's well after midnight.

"Hand in a water cup trick?" I ask.

"You know, to make someone wet the bed." She waves her hand at me and then inspects her nails.

I close the cap on the nail polish. "That doesn't work."

"How do you know?" She swings her legs off my lap and puts them on the floor.

"Putting someone's hand in water won't prevent their body from producing the anti-diuretic hormone, which in turn suppresses your kidneys from excreting urine as you're sleeping."

"Geez, you are such a buzzkill." She yawns and stretches. "I'm exhausted. Can I borrow something to sleep in?"

We head back to my room and I pull out a pair of flannel PJs and hand them to her.

She gapes at them. "You own actual pajamas?"

"Don't you?"

"No. I sleep in ratty shirts or sweats."

"Oh."

We change and brush our teeth. I have a package of spare toothbrushes under my sink in the bathroom that I open up for Freya.

Once we're finished, I head back into my bedroom to find Freya snuggled under the comforter on my queen bed.

"Please don't make me sleep on the sofa bed," she pleads.

I shrug. "You can sleep in here." I climb under the covers on the opposite side and turn off the light on the bedside table.

I've never slept in the same bed as someone else before. I suppose it's a common occurrence for most adolescents to share a sleeping space with your peers. I shift in the smaller space allotted to me and try to get comfortable. I can hear Freya breathing, and feel her shifting on her side as well.

"Lucy?" she whispers.

"Yes?"

"Can I tell you something?"

"Of course. Why are you whispering?"

"Oh. I don't know," she says in a normal voice. "It's about Cameron."

I don't respond, instead waiting for her to continue.

"Remember how I told you that I wouldn't sleep with him and that's when he stopped returning my calls?"

"Yes."

"Well, that wasn't entirely true."

I turn towards her on the bed, lying on my side. I can't see her face very well in the dark; she's just a lump in the darkness on the pillow next to me.

"The truth is," she continues, "well, I *did* tell him I didn't want to sleep with him, but then it happened anyway."

What does she mean? "It happened anyway?" I ask, my voice escalating. "Freya, did he rape you?"

"No," she says quickly. "I mean, not really."

I take a deep breath. "Not really?" Something is building in my chest, another new emotion, foreign and burning. "Freya, if you said no at any point, and he didn't listen..." I don't finish my sentence. I can hear her next to me, sniffing and wiping her face with the sleeve of the flannel long sleeve shirt.

She's crying, but instead of making me panic like it normally does, it makes me want to—

"If I ever see that arrogant, asinine, piece of...shit," I finally say the word. It's awkward on my tongue, but it's the only one that seems to fit in this situation. "I'm going to cut his penis off with a plastic spoon."

A surprised choke of laughter erupts from Freya, shocking her out of her tears.

"Oh, please do." Her laughter and tears subside and then she says, "I don't want to give you any of the gory details. But I did say no, and it didn't stop." She's silent for a moment while I process this, and I try to suppress my own growing anger. The nerve of that man.

"And then he wouldn't return my calls and he did move on to someone else, but instead of being upset I was more...relieved," she says. "Then I saw him, yesterday at the coffee stand over by the library and he acted like nothing had changed." Her voice is quiet in the darkness, a whisper of pain and confusion. "He came up and put his arm around me and called me 'girlie'."

From her tone, I can tell she's rolling her eyes, even though I can't see the motion in the darkness.

"I told him to go fuck himself." She laughs and I find myself chuckling along with her even though I still feel angry and confused on her behalf.

"He was so mad at me. That *I* rejected *him*. Like, oh no, no one could ever not want the great and powerful Cameron." She snorts and I can hear the smile in her voice. "It was very gratifying."

"You did the right thing," I tell her. "You deserve so much better."

"Duh."

"We should contact the authorities," I say after a moment.

"I thought about it. But there's no physical evidence. He didn't hurt me. We had been fooling around before so there wouldn't be any...tearing or anything." She sighs. "It would be a lot of time and work, and in the end it would be my word against his."

I think over what she's saying. It sounds logical but it feels absolutely wrong.

"You know the weirdest part? I feel like," she stops for a moment before continuing, "Like I need to erase his memory. No, not erase. Replace. I want to find someone else. Someone who is the exact opposite of everything that Cameron is and everything he represents. And once I find this paragon, I want to sleep with him a million times until the other memories have faded and are no more than a distant and vague recollection. Is that weird?"

"No. I think whatever you're feeling is completely normal," I say, and I cringe at myself when my voice comes out sounding flat and unemotional. "I'm sorry," I add. "I don't think I can be much help for you right now. I'm still thinking about the different ways I can hurt him without arousing the suspicion of the local authorities."

She laughs. "You are helping, Lucy."

"Forget everything I said about how hiring someone to hurt him was wrong. If anything, it was the best idea you ever had."

We're both silent in the dark room, lost in our own thoughts. I flip over on my back and stare at the glow of moonlight on the ceiling. I've gone from exhausted to wide awake in the last few minutes. I wasn't kidding. I really do want to maim Cameron or beat him within an inch of his life. I've never felt such a violent inclination. I take a deep breath to calm myself and shut my eyes. Why am I so angry? The answer strikes me suddenly, forceful in its own obviousness: I care about Freya. She's my friend and I like her. I don't want her to be hurt in any way, shape or form.

It's very strange.

"Good night Freya," I say.

"Good night Lucy."

Chapter Fourteen

Bad times have a scientific value. These are occasions a good learner would not miss.
                                         —Ralph Waldo Emerson

Tuesday the week of Thanksgiving is freezing cold. It's windy and awful and by the time I'm walking up the steps of the duplex, my ears hurt and I can't feel my nose, despite the large jacket, scarf and hat I threw on when I was leaving.

Jensen steps out of his door just as I'm opening mine. It feels like forever since I've seen him, and he hasn't said one word to me since he saw me with Tony, so instead of entering my much warmer house, I can't help but stop.

"Hi," I say.

"Hey." He locks his door before turning around.

"How are you?" I ask.

"Great." He doesn't sound great. He sounds anxious to get away from me.

"Are you going anywhere for Thanksgiving?" I should just shut up and go inside—I am probably entering the second stage of hypothermia after all—but Jensen has become a sick addiction, and I just need one more fix.

"Yeah, I'm taking the red-eye to my grandparents' place in L.A. tonight."

"I bet it's warmer there." Probably the most unintelligent statement I've ever uttered in my life. "That'll be nice," I add. Nope, that one clinched it.

"Well. I'll see you later," he says before bolting down the stairs.

I'm sure he's in a hurry to get out of the cold. At least, that's what I would like to believe if I wasn't logical enough to consider the truth. The truth is, he doesn't hate me. He probably just feels neutral towards me. Indifference. After a small consideration I realize that's probably worse than hate. Hate at least implies some sort of passion.

This is not rational. I'm going to tell him the truth. He's the one who said he appreciates honesty above all else, especially after what he's been through. I can at least give him that. The entire truth, about Tony and Freya and everything. Maybe then we can go back to how it was before. At the very least we can be friends again.

The wind picks up and blows harder, rattling my windows.

After the holidays. Then I'll come clean.

***

Dull gray light filters through the thin white curtains and rouses me from sleep. I had set my alarm to go off at six thirty in order to catch the bus from campus to my parents' house, but it never went off. It should be dark outside still. I sit up, my eyes flying to the alarm clock, but the normally green digital face is pitch-black. It's unnaturally silent in my room. The power is out.

I get out of bed and head to the kitchen to grab my cell phone and immediately regret leaving the warmth of my comforter. I don't know how long the power's been off, but it's freezing in here. I peek out the window in the kitchen and gasp in shock. There's at least five feet of snow on the ground.

It snows here every winter, but not like this. The town is in a valley surrounded by mountains and when it does snow, it normally dumps at the higher elevations and it will max out at about an inch or two on the valley floor. It very rarely hits us this hard. No wonder the power went out.

My cell phone still has battery life, but just barely. It's eight o'clock in the morning. I quickly dial my mom's number.

"Happy Thanksgiving!" she answers her phone.

"Mom? Thanksgiving is tomorrow."

"Lucy! I know Thanksgiving is tomorrow, but it's the holidays!" she trills in a sing-song voice. A statement that only makes sense in her mind. "Are you okay honey?"

"I'm fine. My power is out and I missed the bus."

"They said on the news there are blackouts all over the city, but don't worry, you just sit tight. Ken and Tom are going to come get you as soon as Doug gets done plowing, but that might not be until tomorrow. I'm sure you'll be fine, you're such a smart girl."

Doug McDougall is our neighbor and he also works for the city. One of his jobs in the winter is running a giant plow truck when it snows.

"Okay. I thought the McDougalls hated us."

"Oh, they do not! You know how the boys are, always playing pranks on each other. It will be fine. Sheila is here with her boyfriend, and the kids have been asking about you since they got here yesterday."

My mom rambles on a bit more about the family that's already there and what's been going on before my phone starts beeping at me.

"Mom?" I have to interrupt her. "My phone's dying. I'll see you tomorrow."

"Love you Lucy!" she says and then the phone cuts off. I pull it from my ear and look at the now black screen. Then I look around my cold, silent apartment.

I eat a slice of pumpkin pie for breakfast because it's the only thing I have that doesn't need to be cooked, and then I get back in bed with a book. The wind is blowing again, rattling the windows and gusting against the thin walls, and it's still snowing.

I can't take a hot shower because there's no power to heat the water. Going to the bathroom is torture, not only because of leaving the sanctuary of my somewhat warm bed, but also the porcelain toilet seat feels like an ice cube against my rear end.

By three o'clock in the afternoon, the power is still off and I fear I'm losing my mind. I have to do something because even my bed is getting cold, despite all the covers and jackets I've thrown on myself. I'm uncomfortable and freezing and bored. And it's just so...quiet. There are no normal sounds. No heater kicking on, no hum of the refrigerator, just the cold wind beating against the walls outside.

If only I had a fireplace like Jensen's, I could at least huddle up in the living room, listening to the crackle of wood, feeling the heat from the flames.

I wonder if Jensen made it to the airport last night.

Maybe he's not here and I could use his fireplace. Surely, he wouldn't deny me such a small luxury. I wouldn't touch anything and I would replenish any firewood used.

And that settles it in my mind. It's better than just sitting here, after all.

I grab a bobby pin from the bathroom to get past the lock if needed, and then I bundle up and head out the door. Ten steps later and I knock first, just in case he's still home, and I'm surprised when it swings open and Jensen hustles me inside shutting us in quickly to block out he cold wind.

"You're home," I say stupidly, shivering, standing in his entryway in my large jacket and PJ pants and slippers. He's wearing black cotton pants and a flannel button-up top.

"Flights were cancelled last night," he says. "Not that I could have driven to the airport in this." His eyes narrow on my face. "You're freezing. Your lips are literally blue."

I nod. No need to waste breath with pointless speaking.

"Come on." He grabs my arm and leads me into the living room. He's pushed back all of his furniture. There's a mattress on the floor in front of the fireplace all covered in blankets.

He helps me take off my jacket and then he lifts the covers up on the bed and shoves me under them, getting in behind me.

"What are you doing?" I ask through chattering teeth.

He wraps his arms around me, and pulls me against him, my back to his front. "What do you think I'm doing? You're the scientist. I have to get you warm and this is the most efficient way to do it."

I don't have a response. Of course he's right. After a few minutes, our combined body heat starts warming both of us up and my shaking stops.

"I didn't realize how cold I was," I say finally. I also didn't realize just how alone I was on my side of the duplex. But lying here, listening to the crack of the wood in the fire and to Jensen's breathing against my neck, just the sounds of normalcy have relaxed something inside me.

"Are you hungry?" he asks after a minute more of lying together.

106

"Starving." I haven't eaten since the slice of pumpkin pie this morning.

He pulls away from me and gets out of the bed, heading for the kitchen and I immediately miss his warmth.

"Do you like hot dogs?" he calls.

"I like anything edible at this point."

He returns a few minutes later with his hands full. He has a package of hot dogs, a bag of buns, a handful of small ketchup packets, two wire coat hangers wrapped in paper from a drycleaner and a pair of pliers.

He sits on the end of the mattress, only a few feet away from the black metal fire grate, and rips the paper off the hangers, throwing it into the fire. Then he straightens the coat hangers out into long metal sticks using the pliers to unwrap the twisted metal. Once that's done, he opens the hot dog package and slides the dogs lengthwise onto the sticks.

I slide out from under the warmth of the blanket to sit next to him. It's much warmer in his house than it was in mine, but it's still a bit chilly, even with the fire. After I situate myself next to him, he hands me one of the dogs on a stick, and moves the grate from the fire. I immediately thrust the food into the flames.

Jensen leans his own stick against the wall and kneels on the bed next to me, pulling the covers towards us. He covers me with the blanket first, then grabs his stick and sits next to me so we are sharing the warmth and roasting our dogs at the same time.

"Thank you," I tell him.

We have to sit pretty close to share the blankets and the fire. His leg is resting against mine. Granted, there are at least two layers of clothes between my skin and his, but it doesn't change the fact that my stomach drops every time one of us moves and his legs rub against mine.

"For what?" he asks.

"This." I lift the stick slightly. "I've never been so excited about processed, nitrate-full meat in my entire life. Also thank you for letting me in."

"No thanks required. What else would I have done? Let you freeze? And this isn't exactly a gourmet meal, here."

I shrug. "It's better than nothing."

It doesn't take long for the dogs to heat through. We help each other with the buns and condiments and sticks until

107

finally we are both eating. I think this cheap hot dog is the most delicious thing I've ever had.

We both have another one and then he puts more wood on the fire before replacing the grate. We get back under the covers, facing each other but not touching.

"You should stay here tonight," he says. The firelight flickers over his face and there's no way I can say no. I'm not sure a ravaging pack of starving warthogs could convince me to return to my cold and desolate side of the duplex. Even though, normally, I'm a fan of isolation.

"Okay," I say.

His phone starts making music and he turns and picks it up from the floor next to the mattress.

"Hello?"

A woman's voice filters through the line.

"Hey, mom. No, everything is fine."

He's quiet and I can hear his mom's voice on the phone, but I can't make out what she's saying.

"Okay, yeah." Pause. "Uh, huh. Right." A longer pause, and finally, "Give everyone my love."

He hangs up and turns back towards me, leaving the phone on the floor.

"Is your mom worried about you?" I ask.

"More likely she's worried about being alone with my dad and his parents," he says.

"Oh. They're in L.A., where you were going?"

"Yeah, they've been there since Monday."

"Do you always spend the holidays there with your family?"

"Mostly. They do it up really nice and my grandparents have this giant house. Except..." He pauses and frowns.

"Except?"

He shrugs, shifting the covers a little. "It's always nice. I mean too nice, too formal. I've always kind of wanted to have Thanksgiving like in the movies. Weird relatives, eating in the living room watching football, kids running around making a mess and driving everyone crazy."

"That sounds like every dinner with my family."

"Yeah?"

"Except my mom follows the kids around with her dust buster and is constantly cleaning. She's a little anal. And my

108

grandma usually gets drunk and starts calling everyone Scooby."

He laughs. "Why does she do that?"

"The world may never know."

We're quiet for a minute, but it's not awkward. We lay there and listen to the crackle and pop of the fireplace. I trace patterns on the soft sheets with my finger.

"Can I ask you something?" he says.

I shift my eyes from my finger to his face. "Of course."

"You haven't, uh, I mean, we haven't talked much lately, and I saw you with that guy Tony that one night, and I was just wondering if you, um, didn't need me anymore? For your research?"

"I..." I can't lie to him. I had planned on telling him the truth, and here's my perfect opening. Especially after that completely awkward and totally sweet bumbling mess of a statement.

But I feel ashamed to reveal the truth. How can I tell him I wanted to make him jealous? That I willfully attempted to hurt him? When the real truth is that I don't want to hurt him at all. Ever.

"I haven't replaced you," I say, finally. "He was one of Freya's friends."

"Oh. Okay." He looks confused.

I sigh and cover my face with a bit of blanket. I can't look at him when I say this. "The truth is," I say into the fabric. "Tony is gay. And Freya said that I should try to make you jealous, and I went along with it even though it's stupid and wrong and I thought for sure when I met him that you would see he prefers men and it wouldn't matter, but I didn't know he was a drama major—"

"Lucy," Jensen interrupts me and tugs the blanket away from my face. "You were trying to make me jealous?"

I watch his expression. There's a glimmer of relief and something else. Amusement?

"I guess so," I say.

"Why?"

My mouth opens and closes. Then opens again. Well. "Because I think I like you?" I don't mean for it to sound like a question, but that's how it pops out of my mouth.

"Are you not sure?" he asks, but one corner of his mouth is sliding upwards, like he knows I'm sure and he knows how hard it is to admit that to someone when you aren't sure if they return your affection and he wants to see me suffer for his own amusement.

"I'm fairly sure," I say.

"Fairly?"

I pretend to consider. "I'm about eighty-three percent sure."

"And the remaining seventeen percent?"

"Fifteen percent undecided and two percent is pure, unadulterated loathing."

He bursts out laughing, and I can't help but smile at his response even though I still feel embarrassed and unsure. He hasn't said he likes me back.

"I'm glad you told me the truth," he says.

"I'm not sure I share that sentiment."

"Well, you should. I have to tell you, after what I've been through, I appreciate the honesty."

I have a feeling he's referring to his ex-girlfriend Chloe, and her relationship with his best friend.

"My turn," I say, after a minute of silence.

"Your turn for what?"

"A question."

"Okay, shoot."

I want to ask how he feels about me and if my emotions are reciprocated, but I'm not sure I can handle a negative reply. If he doesn't feel the same way, I still have to stay here and face him. I can't exactly leave, at least not without threat of frostbite. I also want to ask about what happened with Chloe and Liam, but I fear that might be too personal, so I settle for the next best question.

"Who's the blonde?"

"What blonde?"

"The one that comes here and stays for approximately three hours every week before she leaves."

"Oh, you mean Candice."

"Candice?"

"She's just a friend." He shrugs.

He doesn't elaborate and I don't want to beleaguer the point. If he says she's a friend, she's a friend. I shut my eyes and lay there analyzing everything that just happened. I admitted something very embarrassing, and he didn't say he likes me back but he also didn't cringe away in horror and shock. He didn't explain about Candice and...

I'm not sure what to think at this point. And I almost don't care. I'm warm now, I'm no longer starving, and the exhaustion is creeping in.

"Lucy?"

I open my eyes and find Jensen watching me through half-lidded eyes.

"Good night," he says.

I smile. "Good night."

Chapter Fifteen

I'm old-fashioned and a square. I believe people should not engage in sex too early. They will never forget that first sexual experience, and it would be a pity to just throw it away. So what's the rush? Hug and kiss and neck and pet, and don't rush into a sexual encounter.

—Dr. Ruth

I awake slowly, coming into awareness in bits and pieces. My leg is asleep. It takes me a few more seconds to come to the realization that my leg is asleep because something heavy is on it. There's also a slight breeze wafting over my head in a rhythmic pattern.

I blink my eyes open and all I can see is Jensen's gray cotton shirt right in front of my face. That's not a breeze, that's Jensen breathing. I pull my head back a few inches to try and determine the situation. His face is inches above mine and his eyes are closed. His arm is lying over my midsection and our legs are entangled. How did this happen?

I attempt to extricate myself, but he mumbles something inarticulate and pulls me even closer. Now we're pressed against each other and I can feel the proof against my stomach that men really do wake up in the morning aroused against their own volition. Even though part of me is alarmed, other, more unfamiliar sensations course through me. My stomach flips, my breathing comes out faster and I have the unmistakable urge to get even closer and kiss him, morning breath and all.

No. I take a deep breath and remind myself that I have control over my emotions and body. Nobody controls how I feel except me.

The thoughts fly away as soon as Jensen's hands start moving up and down my back. And then even farther down, cupping my backside and pulling me up a little so his morning stubble scrapes against my face, his lips brushing past mine and heading straight to my neck.

Oh, wow. This is different. His mouth moves down across my neck, to my collarbone and then back up to my ear and down again, nibbling, sucking, kissing, one of those actions is happening at any point, but I'm not really sure on the specifics since my body has suddenly become a haze of sensation.

Still kissing various parts of my body, he gently moves towards me, forcing me to my back in order to settle on top of me between my thighs. He's kissing down my collarbone and lower and lower and even though we are both fully clothed, the position is intimate enough that bolts of pleasure course through my legs and I arch against him and squirm so that his erection hits me right *there* and holy moly nothing has ever felt so—

Music. Jensen's phone is going off next to the bed and it's enough to pull me from the physical spell he's weaving over me. He removes his lips from my body and stares down at me with heavy lidded eyes and an expression that makes me want to throw his phone against the wall hard enough to stop the noise.

"Jensen." Whose breathy voice is that? Surely not mine.

The music stops momentarily only to start up again immediately.

Jensen's groans and his body collapses on top of mine with dead weight for a couple beats before he yanks himself away and leans over the side of the bed to grab his phone.

"Hello?"

I take the moment to gather my thoughts and straighten my clothes. My shirt has somehow ridden up on the bottom to the point where my bra is exposed. How did that happen? I sit on the edge of the bed, my back to Jensen, running my fingers through my long hair, making sure it's not sticking straight up since I slept without a hair tie. Not that I care what I look like. Because I don't. I never do.

"Yeah, Mom. I know. There's no way I can get to the airport today." He sounds a bit aggravated. "Just don't worry about me."

Jensen sits up with the phone still pressed to his ear and turns in my direction, his eyes roving over me. I stop messing with my hair and slink out of the bed and down the hall to the bathroom. I really have to pee.

There's no window. I hit the light switch, but the power is still out. I shut the door, pee in the dark, and when I'm done, open the door to let light in while I wash my hands and attempt to tame my hair.

When I head back to the living room, Jensen is still on the phone, his back to me. I lean awkwardly against the wall at the end of the hallway. I'm not sure I should go anywhere near the bed. It's turned into some kind of vortex of hormones. I might get sucked in and never get out.

"Uh-huh. I love you, too. Bye." He hangs up, sighs, and then as if just remembering I'm around somewhere, his shoulders tense and he spins around. When he sees me lurking in the hallway, he relaxes.

"Do you want breakfast?" he asks.

"More hot dogs?"

He smiles. "I have a better idea."

Fifteen minutes later, we're bundled up and ready to face the outside world. It stopped snowing and the sun is shining, but it's not putting off enough warmth to melt much, if any, of the snow.

I went home to get my winter gear, and when I knock on Jensen's door again, he opens it quickly and steps out, covered head to toe in a beanie, scarf, gloves, jacket and boots.

"Where are we going?" I ask.

He holds up a couple pairs of snowshoes. "We're going for a walk."

Snowshoeing is a lot harder than it looks. For one, you have to step sort of wide and slow and you still sink a little into the snow. There's a bit more resistance than regular walking. So by the time we make it to the end of our alley, I'm panting and sweating inside all my layers of clothes.

"Are we there yet?" I manage between breaths.

114

Jensen is walking slightly in front of me and he turns and flashes me a brilliant smile. "Isn't this great?"

"If you say so."

He turns out of the alley and into the street. It's obvious a snow plow has been through this area. While they successfully cleared the street, they also piled more snow onto the sidewalk, which means we are now muddling through lumpy, hilly snow. I'm watching my feet to make sure I don't end up on my face or rear end when something hits me on the shoulder.

I gasp and look up. Jensen's stopped in front of me, smiling.

"Did you just throw a snowball at me?" I ask.

"Yep," he says, still smiling. "What are you gonna do about it?"

I shrug. "Nothing." I know this game. I have older brothers.

He seems a little disappointed but turns around and we keep moving. It's nearly impossible to sneak up on someone in snowshoes, so after a minute I stop and say, "Hey, I think my shoe is loose, will you help me?"

He walks back to where I am, face serious, and bends over to tighten the shoe. And that's when I shove a handful of snow down the back of his jacket, under his shirt.

He yelps and too late to realize I've miscalculated our positions and his willingness to play in the snow. He's kneeling in front of me at the perfect level to pick me up, and he uses it to his advantage. He shoves his shoulder into my stomach— not painfully, I am too bundled up to feel more than a slight push—and throws me into a cold pile of snow, landing halfway on top of me.

I scream and laugh as he tries and fails to get snow under my clothes.

"How many layers do you have on?" he asks, picking at the small gap at my throat with his thickly gloved fingers.

"Too many," I manage to get out, still laughing as his fingers dig into my sides with enough force to penetrate the thick pad of clothing covering my body.

"Definitely too many," he says, his voice lower than normal and I wish I could see his eyes, but he's wearing sunglasses and so am I. I'm glad for them—the sun hitting the snow is brighter than a camera flash that never goes away—but I want to know what he's thinking.

After a moment of lying on top of me, he stands up awkwardly since he has to position his snow shoes, then he pulls me up and we continue down the block to the corner convenience store.

The store is open, but the shelves are nearly bare. We take off the snow shoes before entering, leaving them against the wall outside. Once inside we grab a few packages of white-powdered and chocolate mini donuts, a bag of chips, some juice and two bags of jerky before heading back out into the snow.

Jensen carries the goods as we shoe back to the duplex.

"Hey. Someone plowed here while we were gone," I say when we turn onto our alley and the four feet of snow that was here less than an hour ago has been shoved to the side.

"Why is the plow still here? And parked in front of our duplex?" He gives me a perplexed look.

"Oh, no." I recognize the dark head leaping from the truck and walking around to head up the stairs to bang on my door.

"What is it?"

I face him and offer a weak smile. "My brothers."

Chapter Sixteen

I have frequently been questioned, especially by women, of how I could reconcile family life with a scientific career. Well, it has not been easy.

— Marie Curie

"Where's Doug?" I ask accusingly when we get in earshot. Not all of my brothers are here. Just Sam and Jon.

Sam smiles at me from the driver's seat of the truck, where the window is down. "Nice to see you, too, sis."

"Doug's at home. We, uh, *borrowed* the plow," Jon says. He's standing on the porch, ostensibly because he was knocking on my door when we approached.

There's no changing them. Borrowed means stolen in their skewed vocabulary.

There's a lot of strange staring and exchanging of looks between Sam, Jon, and Jensen and then nearly simultaneously, all their gazes swing my way.

I sigh. "This is Jensen."

"Jensen, huh?" Sam says, throwing me a cheeky grin.

I shake my head at him in warning because I know exactly what he's thinking.

Jon comes down the steps and shakes Jensen's hand and I can tell he does it with excessive force. Jon keeps his dark hair cut high and tight. He's nearing forty, but he stays in good shape. He's wearing a sweater that reads, "Not as lean, not as mean, but still a Marine."

"Where were you guys?" Jon crosses his arms over his chest and gives me a stern look and then gives the same look to Jensen and then back to me.

"We went to the store for food," I say. His tough guy attitude doesn't fool me, I know him too well.

Jensen dutifully holds up our bag of goods as evidence.

"Well, we're here to get you and take you home," Sam says.

"It was nice to meet you Jensen," Jon says dismissively.

Jensen turns away. He smiles at my brothers, but when he turns away from us, his shoulders slump slightly.

"Wait," I say. I shouldn't do this. For all I know, Jensen is ecstatic to finally be away from me and will probably suffer numerous untold horrors at the hands of my family, but... "I have to get my stuff. And I'm not coming with you unless Jensen's coming too."

"It's okay," Jensen says quickly, glancing from me to Jon and then back again. "You have your family stuff to do and I don't want to intrude."

"It's not okay," I tell him. "The only problem will be if you don't come with us."

Jon puts a heavy hand on my shoulder. "We don't have much room in the truck. It's only a bench seat cab."

I stick out my chin. "Give me your phone," I say to Jon.

"Really?"

I raise my eyebrows and he complies with a sigh.

I call the house and when mom answers I tell her about Jensen being all alone with no power and how I've invited him over and he's refused. Then I hand the phone over to Jensen.

Five minutes later, we're all in the plow. He wasn't kidding, there's just one bench seat and I'm stuffed in between Sam and Jon. Poor Jensen is between Jon and the window and I wonder if he regrets being forced into this situation. I can't apologize or say anything to check on him, though, because Sam is making me shift for him at times since the stick is between my legs and we're all crammed into the small space.

"So. Jensen," Sam says. He guns it while getting on the freeway, which has been mostly plowed already so he raises the scooper up front with the touch of a button on the dash. "What are you in school for?"

"Law."

"A lawyer, huh?" Jon asks. "That's what you want to do with your life?"

"I'm studying civil rights," Jensen says.

"Oh." There's a moment of silence, punctuated by the rumble of the large truck.

"What are your intentions with Lucy?" Sam asks, finally.

"Sam!" I try to jab him in the side with my elbow, but he anticipates the move and blocks me with his arm.

"You don't have to answer that, Jensen," I say.

"I don't mind," he says. I can't see him around Jon's big head, but he sounds calm and fairly comfortable with the situation. As comfortable as one could, I suppose. "I don't really have any intentions. Lucy is a smart, funny, kind person whom I enjoy spending time with. Anything else is up to her."

I smile at his response.

It doesn't stop. The entire drive—which takes nearly an hour—Sam and Jon relentlessly grill Jensen on various items of interest and torture. Past girlfriends, does he have a job, what's his family like, why he's letting his parents pay for his education and not being a real man and taking care of it himself, and on and on it goes. Jensen does a great job holding his own. When they get too personal or out of line, he tells them it's none of their damn business. Which puts them off, for a minute. When we finally pull into the circular driveway, I can't get out fast enough.

Someone's shoveled the drive, and it's still a little slippery, but I make it into the house unscathed, the boys lagging a bit behind me.

I brace myself before opening the door, ready for the chaos that awaits and I'm not disappointed. Immediately, a stream of at least six children somewhere between the ages of five and ten flash past me in the entry way, running from the dining room to the living room screaming and trailing a flood of apple juice, fruit snacks (and is that toilet paper?) behind them.

"Wow," Jensen says from behind me. "You weren't kidding."

"You asked for it," I respond before Sam and Jon come in behind us.

Jon slams the door and Sam yells, "Honey, we're home!"

No one responds to our entrance. Jon and Sam skirt around us and head into the living room where I can hear

119

football and my Dad yelling at the TV combined with other male voices, probably my Uncle Roger and my other brothers.

I don't wish to disturb the testosterone levels in there, so I head in the opposite direction. Jensen follows behind me as we head through the dining room and into the kitchen to meet my mom and find out where she wants us before I show him to his room.

The kitchen is yellow and warm and it smells delicious. The room is packed with people sitting in the breakfast nook, at the bar and standing around the island. There's food everywhere: nuts, crackers, cheese spreads, dips, little quiches, and dinner hasn't even started yet. My mom is a whirling dervish of activity, alternately cleaning up and throwing things in one oven or the other while drinking a glass of wine.

When she sees us she stops what she's doing and comes over to give me a big hug.

"This must be Jensen," she says, all smiles and then she hugs him too.

His eyes are a bit alarmed as they meet mine over her shoulder and I just shrug.

"I'm so glad we convinced you to come!" she says as she pulls back, still holding on to his shoulders.

"How could I refuse," he says. I'm sure he means it. My mother is a force of nature when she wants something, and she always wants to take care of people.

I can't hear what else she says to him because suddenly I'm surrounded by family and friends all hugging and asking about school, something I definitely don't want to talk about, so I evade the questions and turn the subject around to what they have going on. That always works. Once the family talk filters away from me, I move to ask Mom where she wants Jensen to sleep tonight, but she's introducing him to everyone and I have to wait until she's done.

When things calm down, she tells me to put him in the den and I lead him up the stairs.

I point out the bathroom and then his room down the hall.

"I get my own room?" he asks, tossing his backpack onto the bed. The question is probably on his mind because of the mob of people downstairs. My parents couldn't possibly be accommodating everyone.

"Yes. My brothers all live nearby, with the exception of Ken. Most of the people here are staying with them. Only

Grandma's staying here tonight, besides us, and she has the guest room."

"Where are you sleeping?"

I flush, the mention of sleeping reminds me of last night, and I'm suddenly inundated with images of waking up in his arms and what happened directly after.

"In my old room."

His eyebrows lift. "Can I see it?"

"Okay."

He follows me down the hall to my room. The house is fairly big, five bedrooms and three and a half bathrooms.

My room is the last one on the left. I feel a little anxious bringing him in here, but I'm not sure why. I flick on the light and the lamp in the corner turns on and illuminates my old bedroom. Most of the stuff is as it was when I left, but now there's an elliptical in the corner next to my telescope and some of my mom's sewing stuff and books litter the dresser.

He walks in and I follow him, taking my bag off and putting it on the bed. There's a poster of Albert Einstein with his tongue sticking out on one of the walls and he stops to look at it.

"A little more whimsical than I imagined you would like," he says.

I shrug, feeling awkward.

I watch him as he rambles around a little bit more. He points at my bed and says, "That's an interesting quilt."

It's a colorful mess of different shapes and sizes of squares.

"That's my science quilt," I say. "My mom made it based on this chart." I lead him over by the window where the chart is hanging.

"It's part of a computation called 'Capturing Phase Dynamics of Circadian Clocks.' Mom thought it would make a perfect blanket since circadian rhythm is part of the sleep cycle."

He leans next to me to get a good look at the chart. We're only about a foot apart when he turns and faces me.

"Interesting."

There's a pause where we just stare at each other. The light is dim with just the corner lamp on, and his eyes are dark and heavy.

"I'm glad you mentioned the bed," I say, finally.

"Are you?" he asks with a small smile. His eyes drop to my mouth.

I take a step away and yank the blankets and pillows off my bed, chucking them on the floor.

"What are you doing?" he asks.

"Checking for things left behind from my brothers."

"Things?"

"They like to play practical jokes. You should really check your room before you go to sleep because you never—here it is!" My thoughts halt as I pull out a rubber snake coiled under my pillow and throw it at Jensen.

He seems a bit surprised, but he catches it in one hand. "That's...very interesting," he says, holding the offensive item up for inspection.

I yank the sheet down and reach my hand in, pulling out a water balloon.

"A balloon?"

"Water balloon." I shake it so he can hear the water sloshing inside. "With the hopes that I'll lie on top of it and it'll break and appear as if I've wet the bed."

"Oh, okay." He nods in understanding.

"We may be able to use this later," I say, inspecting the balloon in my hand.

"For what?"

"Retribution," I say. What other answer is there?

"The snow down my shirt is starting to make sense now."

Just then, the door flies open and Sam lunges into the room. "A-HA!" he yells pointing towards me.

Jensen and I stare at him.

"Oh," Sam says. His eyes roam from me, by the bed, to Jensen who is halfway across the room and he leans against the wall in a relaxed pose, as if he didn't just jump into my room like he was expecting to interrupt something nefarious.

"I see you found your offerings," Sam says, nodding to the balloon I'm still holding.

"Yes," I say. "I'm trying to determine how I can use this to my advantage."

"I've got a better idea," Sam says with an evil grin.

"What's that?"

He stands up straight and rubs his hands together with undisguised glee. "You know how Ken always passes out after dinner?"

I manage to get out of an uncomfortable dinner situation by volunteering to sit at the kids' table. My mom set up the food buffet style, so after I've filled my plate, I sit in the breakfast nook with the children while the rest of the adults, including Jensen, converge in the formal dining room.

"Is Jensen your boyfriend?" my six-year-old niece Katie asks.

So much for avoiding that question.

"No," I answer quickly. "Well, technically, he's a boy and he's my friend so in that sense of the word yes. But otherwise, no."

She looks at me blankly.

"Do you have kids?" This from Tom's young son David. I think he's four. He watches me, waiting for an answer while he licks the butter off of his bread roll.

"No," I say.

"Why not?"

I think about it for a few seconds. It's on the tip of my tongue to respond with a scientific answer about insemination and the reproductive cycle, but I'm not sure Tom would appreciate that. "Because I'm not married," I say finally.

"Do you like kids?" Katie again.

"I like you," I answer.

"Why aren't you married?" she asks.

That's when Jensen decides to make an appearance, plate in hand. "Is there room for me in here?"

I scoot over and he sits next to me in the booth and starts shoveling food in.

"Can't stand the heat?" I ask him.

"Sam," he says, shaking his head and trying to finish chewing the food in his mouth before continuing.

I save him the trouble. "Put a pea in his nose?" I ask.

Jensen looks at me sharply.

"While everyone was saying what they're thankful for?" I continue.

"How did you know that?" he asks.

123

"The old food in the nose trick. It's a classic. My brothers have been doing it to each other since we were kids, trying to see who will break first and get my dad to yell."

"Can I put a pea in my nose?" David asks.

"No," Jensen and I say at the same time. We smile at each other before continuing the meal.

After dinner we end up in the living room. The TV is on and football is over. Now we're watching some Christmas cartoon movie and most of the kids have congregated under blankets and pillows on the floor. I'm on the couch with Jensen, Sam between us. Ken is in the recliner and Tom disappeared with his wife, as they are inclined to do when they have a moment of free time and babysitters aplenty.

Dinner was good, as it always is, and I'm spared having to help with the dishes by a bevy of relatives who insist on providing relief for my mom in the kitchen.

"Where's my little Scooby?" Grandma says from the wide entrance into the living room.

"Which Scooby is she referring to?" Sam asks me quietly out of the corner of his mouth.

"How am I supposed to know?" I ask in a normal volume.

We're spared figuring out drunken Grandma's request because one of the kids gets up off the floor and runs to her.

"She literally had six martinis at dinner," Sam says.

"How is she still alive?" Jensen asks.

"The world may never know," Sam says, shaking his head. "Ken has a theory that she's a reanimated corpse."

"Sam!" I scold.

"What?" He looks offended. "It's Ken's theory, not mine!"

A snore emanates softly from the recliner.

"Speaking of the devil. He's out!" Sam says, again in sotto voice.

"How, exactly, are you planning on getting him into the car?" Jensen asks, whispering.

Sam turns towards him and I can hear the grin in his voice. "You look strong."

***

"I can't believe you're making me film this," I say.

124

"Just shut up and get ready," Tom says from the driver's seat. I'm in the front passenger seat of his sedan, sitting next to him with a smart phone in camera mode, trained behind us. They've placed Ken in the middle of the backseat, Jensen on one side, Sam on the other.

Ken's still miraculously asleep. He's been this way since he was a child, according to my parents. He'll sleep anywhere and it's nearly impossible to wake him once he's out. Add to that the tryptophan from the turkey and the fact that all my brothers have been drinking since lunch, and you have a recipe for disaster. Or a possibly the best prank ever.

We start at the end of the street, Sam insisting on gathering as much speed as possible.

"You guys ready?" Tom asks.

"Yep," Jensen says.

"Ten-four," Sam says.

I sigh.

Tom grins at me and starts driving the car down the road, gathering speed as we go before careening down the driveway and braking suddenly, sending everyone jolting. That's when we all start screaming.

Ken is lurched awake to a car full of screaming lunatics, now only inches from the closed garage door.

"What the fuck!" he yells, his eyes wide and panicked and all caught on film.

The boys immediately start laughing and as soon as Ken realizes what they've done and that the car is no longer in motion, he starts doling out punches to arms and legs. Jensen and Sam attempt to restrain his flailing limbs in between bouts of laughter.

Then Dad opens the driver's door. "What are you kids doing?"

Tom is laughing too hard to respond, so I hold up the phone. "We caught it on camera. Want to watch?"

Chapter Seventeen

Science never solves a problem without creating ten more.

— George Bernard Shaw

After the prank, we all head back inside and share the video with the rest of the family. After that, there's more talking, dessert and coffee. Only when the kids have all passed out on the living room floor and wherever they could cram on couches, do people start to leave.

I hug all of my brothers good-bye. Ken is still a little upset about the whole car thing, but he seems to be getting to the point where he can laugh at himself, too.

After saying goodbye to a multitude of relatives and getting ready for bed, I'm upstairs reading when Mom comes in to say good night.

"Did you have a nice time, honey?"

"Yes." I put the book face down on my lap. "It was good."

"How about Jensen?"

I frown. "I think so."

She nods. "You might want to check the usual places in his room before he goes to bed. He doesn't know how sneaky your brothers can be."

"I think he's getting the idea."

"Plus, it gets colder in the den since it's over the garage. You should bring him some extra blankets in case he gets cold." She walks in the room and sets a folded blanket down at the foot of my bed.

"Okay," I say. Is my mother encouraging me to go see Jensen by myself in a room with a bed at night? What is this world coming to?

She leaves with a smile and a good night and I sit there for a second, dumbfounded. They must really like him. I should probably disabuse her of the notion that we're together, because that's obviously what she's thinking.

I get out of bed and grab the blanket and head down the hall to the den.

The door is slightly ajar, and there's a light on. I knock gently before opening the door.

He's sitting on the side of the bed, looking down at something in his hands.

"Hey," he says, smiling at me. He's back in his flannel pajama pants and the soft gray shirt from last night.

"I brought you an extra blanket," I say. I don't want to lurk in the doorway, so I walk in and sit next to him on the bed, setting the blanket next to me. "What are you doing?"

"Looking at postcards. I found them in the bottom of my bag where I've been throwing them and trying to forget they exist. Liam has been sending them to me since he left." He hands me the stack of cards and I take them carefully. They're photographs that have been turned into post cards. There's the Leaning Tower of Pisa, the Eiffel Tower, Big Ben, and other various locations around Europe. But they all have one glaring thing in common.

"What's the orange circular object in all the photos?"

It looks like a small bean bag or something, but with eyes.

"That is the orange head."

"Orange head," I repeat.

He smiles. "Have you ever seen the movie *Amelie*? It's a French film."

I shake my head. "No."

He takes a deep breath before continuing. "It's about a woman named Amelie. After her mom dies, her dad is kinda reclusive. He's never travelled, but he's always wanted to. Amelie has a friend who's a stewardess, and Amelie gives her a garden gnome from her dad's front yard. The stewardess takes pictures all around the world of the gnome in different countries at various famous sites, and Amelie leaves them for her dad to find."

"Okay."

"The orange head is our garden gnome. But really, it's Liam trying to make amends."

"For Chloe?"

"Yeah."

"Is it working?"

"I don't know." His eyes meet mine in the dim light, and a frisson of tension pulses in the air between us. "You're really lucky," he says, changing the subject. "Your family is amazing."

I'm surprised, after all the pranks and shenanigans that have been going on all day, that he would be able to express anything positive about them.

"They're a little over the top," I say.

"But they love you."

"Yes. I'm sure they do."

"They stole a snow plow to come get you," he reminds me.

"That is true. But I've always felt out of place with them. They're loud and spontaneous. All of the pranks they pull...they're very ridiculous. It's like I was adopted."

"You shouldn't worry about being out of place. They're your family and they love you. Just be yourself."

"I couldn't be any other way."

He watches me for a second with those dark eyes that only look green in the light, and I suppress a shiver.

"You really couldn't be any other way." His hand is on my knee and he's facing me. "It's one of the things I really like about you. There's no prevarication. No deception. No hiding what you're thinking. Except for that whole thing with Tony, but even then..."

His hand on my knee begins to travel upward. I don't quite realize I'm leaning towards him until I'm so close I can see the small crease in his bottom lip. He inclines in my direction and I shut my eyes, waiting.

He lets out a small groan and leans back.

"We can't," he says.

My eyes fly open in time to see the expression of frustration on his face.

"We're in your parent's house and...They've been so great, you should probably leave. Because I know what happens when we kiss and we can't do that here." He scoots away from me, towards his pillow. "I'll just sit on my hands over here and you should run away. Quickly."

128

I can't help the grin that grows on my face. Now, I feel slightly better about my own loss of control around Jensen since it seems he shares the same difficulty.

"Quite the gentleman," I tell him as I stand.

"Yep." He's not looking at me.

"Good night," I say, hand on the doorknob. "Watch out for mousetraps when you're putting your hand in drawers. Or under your pillow. Or anywhere a mousetrap can fit."

He gives me a bemused smile. "Okay."

I watch him for a brief moment. He looks so enticing in the bed with his rumpled hair and dark eyes. I force myself to look away before stepping into the hallway and shutting the door gently behind me.

Once I can't see Jensen anymore, and I'm safely ensconced in my childhood room, my brain starts whirring into action. This means he likes me, doesn't it? Well, I've established that I like him, but what does he think? He's never stated anything specific. Am I just a product of convenience and proximity, or is this going somewhere?

Oh dear. I'm turning into a girl.

I shove the emotion-fueled thoughts out of my mind.

Does it really matter? The most important part of this is that I'm happy. He's happy. I'm having fun. I'm accomplishing precisely what I set out to obtain – emotions. I like that Jensen fits in well with my family. He goes along with their absurd antics, he's a gentleman in my mother's house, and he's fun to be around.

I climb into bed, moving the sheets aside, pausing for a moment to remove a plastic piece of fake vomit and toss it on the dresser.

Actually, I feel a little remorse about my own judgmental attitude towards my family and their antics. Jensen thinks I'm lucky; as a matter of fact, he wishes he had a family as ridiculous as my own. Maybe...maybe they aren't so ridiculous.

Chapter Eighteen

Nothing shocks me. I'm a scientist.
                    –Indiana Jones

The day after Thanksgiving, we have a giant breakfast of fruits, meats, bagels, and almost any other breakfast food you could possibly imagine because my mom can't do anything by half. After that, Jensen is loaded down with leftovers—for some reason, I get nothing—and we are loaded into Sam's truck to be taken home.

The plow was returned to its rightful owner at some point the day before, and the roads have been mostly cleaned. The snow has melted enough that the streets are drivable.

Sam drops us off in front of the duplex and takes off, leaving us alone on the porch.

"Well." Jensen shrugs his backpack on. "I guess I'll see you later?"

"Yes," I say, while searching for my keys in my bag. "Bye," I call out over my shoulder before unlocking my door and entering my side of the duplex.

I've just tossed by bag on the couch and I'm checking the power—it works, thankfully—when there's a knock at the door.

I open it and Jensen is standing with his hands in his pockets, rocking back on his heels.

"So," he says. "Do you have any plans later?"

"I just got home, how could I have made plans already?"

He laughs. "Right. Would you like to come over for dinner later? I have some delicious leftovers." He offers with a shrug and a smile. "Maybe we could watch a movie?"

"Okay."

"Okay. So at like five?"

"Okay."

"Okay, I'll see you then." He steps backwards and nearly trips over a slightly raised board in the deck and then laughs at himself.

I smile, but I feel a little confused by the whole conversation and I shut the door before he gets back into his place.

That was weird. Was he nervous?

***

I spend most of the day catching up on my e-mails and cleaning. I'm ready and hungry by four thirty, so I head over to Jensen's.

He answers the door and says, "You're early," before stepping back to let me in. It's still cold outside, and he shuts the door quickly. The mattress is no longer in the living room, but there's still a fire going in the fireplace.

I shrug. "I didn't have anything else to do, and I'm hungry."

"I've never looked forward to leftovers so much in my life. Your mom is an amazing cook."

"I guess when you've raised four boys you learn how to cook big meals."

"Make yourself comfortable," he says. "I'm going to throw our plates in the oven."

"Okay." I sit on the couch. There's a DVD case on the coffee table. I pick it up.

"Is this what we're watching?" I call out.

He sticks his head out of the doorway separating the kitchen from the living room and grins. "Yep."

We watch the movie, eating our leftover plates in the living room and sitting on the floor.

When it's over, Jensen shuts it off and turns to me. "So?"

We couldn't talk much while it was playing since it's subtitled.

I think it over a little. "I liked it. I liked that Amelie is an introvert, but it doesn't stop her from trying to help people. It made me feel happy for her, at the end. It's interesting how movies instigate emotions in us."

"She reminds me of you," he says. "Her curiosity, her need to understand and help others. Her eyes."

I'm not sure how to respond so I stand and start cleaning up. I help him put the dishes in the dishwasher, a task we do mostly in silence, only breaking it occasionally to discuss various parts of the movie and then we end up back in the living room.

"Can I ask you a question?" I ask, when we're seated next to each other on the couch, our knees only inches apart.

"Of course."

"You don't have to answer if you don't want to."

"Well, if I don't want to, then I won't. Go ahead."

"Will you tell me about Chloe?" I ask.

He stretches his legs out in front of him and leans back a little on the couch next to me, settling in. "What do you want to know?" he asks.

"Anything you're willing to share."

"More of your research?" he asks.

"Partly," I admit.

He searches my eyes for a long moment and then nods. "We grew up together. We lived next door to each other, and when we were little, our parents would put us together if one of our nannies was sick." He shrugs and takes a breath and thinks for a few seconds before continuing. "I used to find frogs in the pond in front of my house and try to scare her with them, but she would just pick them up and put them back outside and scold me for taking them from their home." He laughs at this. "Then when we started school, we were best friends until around middle school. That's about the time when we both started finding friends our own gender, and hanging out so much became a little awkward. But, we were still friends, and then it just...changed into something more."

I can see that he's thinking again and I stay silent, waiting for him to continue.

"I was fourteen and we went to the beach house. Her parents own a house in Northern California, right on the

132

ocean. It was the summer before our sophomore year of high school, and it was the first year she wore a bikini. That's when I noticed she was turning into a woman and was no longer the annoying girl who used to make me attend all her goldfish funerals. She was no longer a child or a gawky middle-schooler. At some point between eighth grade and age fifteen, we both changed. I remember thinking she was beautiful."

"That's when you started dating?"

"No." He smiles at me. "I had to chase her a bit. But we were friends, good friends. And then one night after a school dance, we were making nachos in her kitchen and I kissed her."

I wonder for a minute what that would be like. Having someone so close to you and then falling from friendship into romance. I can't really picture it.

"When did you know that you loved her?" I ask.

He sighs and leans his head back against the back of the chair, looking up at the ceiling. "You see, that's the weird thing. Looking back, I'm not sure I ever did. At least, not in the way a man should love a woman he's dating. I still love her, and I will always care about her, despite everything, but it's more like how you feel for a sister or something."

"But at the time, you thought you were in love with her?"

"Oh, yeah. The thing with Chloe though, there was always some part of her she held back. It felt like...like she didn't fully trust me or something. I don't know how to explain it. I showed her everything, every bleak and broken part of myself, but there was always something missing on her side." There's a pause and then he says, "Her dad died when we were sixteen. It was tough, for a long time. Her mom became really controlling, not wanting anything to happen to the only person she had left and it sort of smothered her. Eventually, Chloe wanted to find a way to escape and she sent out all kinds of signals that she needed help, but I was too caught up in my own life and my own problems to pay attention. But Liam noticed.

"And that wasn't the only part of our problems, really. I think that we were together for so long, I didn't know how to be by myself. We both probably didn't know how to be alone. And our parents were ecstatic about us being together. They practically planned the wedding when we were born. Her dad loved me, and then he died and neither of us wanted to

133

disappoint anyone. Then, with Chloe and Liam..." He stops and clears his throat. "When everything changed it was—" he breaks off. "I don't know. I hope that Chloe really loves him and that she wasn't just looking for a way out."

"A way out of what?"

"Us. Her mom. Her life. Everything."

I think about what he's said. It would be strange, to be so close to someone, but not. "If her feelings for you had changed, why didn't she just tell you?" I ask.

"Very good question. But that's the thing, I don't think her feelings had changed. I don't think she ever loved me. And looking back, I think she was terrified to hurt me and to disappoint her mom. But of course, it ended up being much worse than just breaking up. I lost my two best friends in one fell swoop."

"You don't think you'll be friends again, someday?" I ask.

He shrugs. "I don't know. I hope so."

We're both quiet for a second and he shifts a little, leaning towards me.

"Your turn."

"Okay." I clasp my hands together in my lap and wait for his question.

"You've never been in a serious relationship?" he asks.

"No. I've never been in any relationship."

"What about the science camp guy you told me about before?"

"What about him?"

"You said you'd kissed him."

"Yes. It wasn't serious. There were no emotions involved, it was purely experimental."

"And?"

"And nothing." I shrug. "We were both curious about kissing and other things and we tried it. It was very clinical and scientific."

"That sounds horrible."

"It wasn't great," I agree.

"Wait. Other things? What 'other things' did you do?" He seems fascinated. Since he's shared so much of himself, I suppose I can give him this. It doesn't bother me to share.

"You know," I say. "Intercourse."

His mouth drops open. "You had sex with him?"

"Yes."

He stares at me, open mouthed, before leaning back on the couch. "So, you just slept with him?"

"Yes." I repeat. "It wasn't a big deal."

"I guess not."

He seems upset, but I'm not really sure why.

"It doesn't bother you?" he asks finally.

"What?"

"That your first time wasn't with someone you, you know, love?"

"I'm twenty years old and I have yet to fall in love. If I waited for that, I could be waiting forever. Besides, you just admitted you never really loved Chloe. So really, we're no different."

He's silent at that. I'm watching him, but he's not meeting my eyes.

"Jensen," I say finally.

His wary gaze meets mine.

"You were with Chloe for," I remember his words and do the math in my head quickly. Fifteen to twenty-one. "Six years. You had sex, right?" I can't believe I'm asking this question. Of course they did. Even I—socially stunted as I am—know that people don't engage in a romantic relationship for that long without having sex.

He still doesn't say anything. He puts his hands over his face and takes a deep breath before removing them and looking straight at me.

"No," he says. "We never had sex."

Now it's my turn to be shocked.

"We did other things," he adds, but it barely registers.

"No," I say.

"Yes."

"But you've had sex since your relationship terminated, right?"

There's a very brief pause. "No."

"But, what about Law School Lothario?" I ask, louder than I intend to.

"What?" He chuckles.

"Freya told me you've been a total playboy since you and Chloe broke up. So much so that you're known as the Law School Lothario. And how could...how could you have been together for so long and...it just, it doesn't make sense." The next words shoot out without running through the filter that

135

supposedly exists between the brain and the mouth. "How could she resist you?"

He smiles at that and leans back against the couch, arm stretching out on the top of the sofa behind my head. "Well, when you put it like that." He offers me a charming grin.

"But you must have been with someone since Chloe."

"No. Well, I went on a couple of dates, but nothing happened." He sighs and his head thumps back against the couch. "I can't believe I told you that." His grin slips and he leans towards me, arm still behind my head, fingers now brushing my hair.

I shake my head. "It's nothing to be ashamed of. I'm just surprised."

"Chloe told me, when she told me about Liam, that she never felt the way about me that she feels with him. She's always thought of me as a brother, and I guess you don't want to have sexual relations with brothers." He gives me a pointed look.

"Definitely not."

"Whenever things got physical between us, she would pull away and I didn't mind, we were so young when we first got together. And then her dad died and we were almost never affectionate with each other. I mean, not in a sexual way. She needed someone to hold her more than she needed sex."

He chuckles softly and leans his head back on the couch, looking up towards the ceiling. "Ah, man."

"What's humorous?"

"This is probably the most emasculating conversation I've ever had in my life."

"Why? Because you're a virgin and I'm not?"

"That's exactly why."

A thought strikes me, and I have to clench my jaw to keep the words from popping out of my mouth.

Unfortunately, Jensen notices my efforts. "What is it?" he asks.

"You don't have to be a virgin." I can't quite meet his eyes while I'm speaking, but when I've finished my sentence I meet his eyes.

"What are you saying, Lucy?"

I've never done anything by half in my entire life, and I'm not about to start now.

136

"I'm saying." I slide over to him so our sides are pressed together and I reach up with one hand, placing it gently on his cheek and guiding him to look at me. "I've never felt this attraction with anyone else. Ever. And I would love to have sex with you."

His eyebrows lift, and he smiles at me. Then he bursts out laughing.

My hand is jarred from his face and I frown. "Why is that funny?"

"I have no idea, it just is. You never say what I expect."

"Oh." I don't think it's very funny. At first I'm not sure why I feel upset. But then I realize it's because I've been rejected. "You don't want to have sex with me?" I ask.

His smile falls and his eyes roam over my face. "Lucy," he says seriously. "That's not it at all." He leans towards me, cupping my face in his hands, running his thumbs over my cheeks. "I would love to have sex with you," he says, looking straight into my eyes. A glimmer of humor enters his eyes again. "But not tonight."

"Why not?" I don't understand. He's a male, I'm a female. It's simple biology. And his biology should make him the one convincing me, not the other way around.

His hands slide from my face and he leans back against the couch and watches me for a moment. Then he stands. "Come with me." He holds out his hand and I take it.

He pulls me up gently from the couch and leads me down the hall. His duplex is set up like mine, only in reverse. We pass the master bedroom. The door is open, and I peek in. His bedroom is decorated much like the rest of the house, black and gray, sleek lines and fashionable accessories. He stops outside the closed door to the second bedroom and turns towards me.

"I want to show you something," he says.

"Okay," I say carefully.

He smiles at my tone. "Don't worry, this isn't where I keep dead bodies or mutilated kittens or anything."

"Well, that's a relief."

He grins at me and then pushes open the door and flicks on the light.

My mouth drops open. It's not a spare bedroom or office or anything I expected. The multitude of bright lights running along the ceiling reveal an art studio. He has a desk with a tilted top and an array of utensils, mostly pencils and charcoal, but it's the items hanging on the walls and resting on the floor that catch my attention. The artwork is exactly like what we saw at the art exhibit. The last one. The best one that didn't have an artist name on display.

"You're the artist. The one that we saw." I turn and face him.

He's watching me with almost nervous anticipation.

He takes a deep breath. "Yep."

My brain starts clicking things into place. "This is a secret because of your parents," I say. I face the array of items on display in front of me.

"Yep," he says again. "If my father found out I was still drawing...who knows what he would do. Cut me off, for sure. I'm only able to pursue my passion because my tuition and living expenses are paid for."

"You don't need his money to be able to do this," I tell him in a murmur because my focus is taken by the largest canvas resting against the wall. It's nearly as tall as me and the subject appears familiar.

I move to examine it closer.

"Actually, I do. Art supplies are ridiculously expensive," Jensen says from behind me.

"This is amazing," I say, gesturing to the portrait. It's a woman, half clothed, some kind of soft-looking cloth covering parts of her body, but keeping her legs exposed. One of her legs is disfigured, and the skin looks wrinkled like she was severely burned at some point, but the rest of her is nearly perfect. It's like the Venus de Milo, but instead of missing limbs, they are merely scarred.

"Thank you. That's Candice. Remember, you asked me about the girl who comes over sometimes?"

The light comes on. The blonde. The leggy blonde. The one Freya thought was a hooker.

"Oh," I say. The night of the power outage. I told him I liked him, then I asked him about the female whom I had seen going into his house. Candice. She's just a friend, he said, and I didn't request further clarification.

"Now you know why she keeps coming over." He comes up behind me, wrapping his arms around my middle. "Now that you know my secret," he says in my ear. "You can't tell anyone."

138

"I wouldn't," I say.

"I know. I trust you," he says. "It's weird. I never thought I would trust anyone again."

I smile. We're still facing the portrait. I turn in his arms and look up at him.

"I should go," I say.

"Stay with me."

I search his eyes. "Are you sure? You said earlier that you didn't want to have sex."

He laughs. "I'm not asking you to stay so we can have sex." He shrugs and looks bashful. "I just enjoy your company. Is that weird?"

"Yes."

"And why is that weird?"

I shrug. "I'm not very exciting."

"Says the woman who's propositioned me to be her love slave twice since I've known her."

I feel heat creeping across my face. "Love slave is a slight exaggeration. Besides, that isn't an enjoyable trait. Reeks more of desperation."

"Well." He takes my hand and pulls me gently from the room, flicking the light off and shutting the door behind us. "I enjoy it, so maybe I'm the weirdo in this scenario."

"Maybe you are."

He gives me a large t-shirt to sleep in and a spare toothbrush—even though my own personal items are no more than twenty feet away—and within minutes we are ready for bed.

"I feel slightly underdressed," I say once the lights are off and we're spooning, my back to his front in his large comfortable bed.

I'm still in just a t-shirt, and he has flannel pants and a shirt on.

"If I don't keep myself contained, things might happen that we're not ready for."

"*You're* not ready for," I clarify.

His chest vibrates against my back as he laughs and then we fall quiet.

I think I might have difficulty going to sleep while half my body is touching someone else. For a few minutes, all I can think about is his heartbeat, the feeling of his chest rising and falling next to me, and the sound of his breathing as he falls asleep.

But miraculously, somehow, when I least expect it, I fall.

Chapter Nineteen

Science may have found a cure for most evils; but it has found no remedy for the worst of them all – the apathy of human beings.

—Helen Keller

The rest of the week and Saturday pass in a blur of Jensen and sleeping and eating and more Jensen. I take him to the archery range and he takes me back to the art exhibit. His relationship with the art gallery owner makes more sense now that I know about his artistic pursuits.

By Sunday morning, I'm sure he must be sick of me, but he calls me only an hour after I get home from his place. We've spent the last couple of nights in his bed, doing nothing more than kissing and snuggling despite my best efforts to the contrary.

"What are you doing right now?"

I stare down at my hastily jotted notes. I had been working on my experiment. Or trying to. I feel like an idea on how to study emotional pathogens is hovering under the surface of my mind. Every time I attempt to pull it out, it stays just out of reach. The harder I try to catch it, the more slippery it becomes.

"Nothing," I say.

"My parents invited us over for brunch. Can you come?" He sounds nervous.

"Right now?" I glance over at the clock. It's nine fifty-seven.

"Yeah. Unless you have something else going on," he adds quickly.

"No," I say quickly. "That sounds fine."

A few minutes later, he's knocking at the door.

"Are you ready?" he asks when I open it.

He's wearing a button-up shirt underneath a leather jacket and instead of the jeans I'm used to seeing him in, he's wearing dark slacks and shiny black shoes.

I glance down at myself. I'm wearing stretchy, comfortable jeans, a plain red sweater and sneakers. "Should I change?" I ask.

"No." He gives me a small smile. "You look perfect."

After grabbing my jacket, we get in his already running car—he started it before coming to my door to warm it up before we left—and he pulls out of the spot and down the alley.

"I should probably warn you," he says, when we're getting on the freeway. "My parents aren't like your parents."

"I know."

"I mean, they're really serious."

"I can be serious," I assure him.

That makes him laugh, a little bit. "I know you can, it's just—" he breaks off. "They're not very affectionate. Or approachable."

"Okay."

We drive in silence as he exits the freeway and drives up a long street, the houses and property getting progressively larger the farther we go. Finally, he pulls down a gravel driveway lined with snow-covered trees. The road leads to a gate, an imposing black gate with a large golden letter "W" directly in the middle of it. I look out my window. The gate seems to extend around the property. Jensen rolls down his window and pushes various buttons on a panel. Something beeps and the gate swings open. We drive through the gate, down the road a little further and finally to a circular drive in front of a very large house. The outside is brick and the entrance is shadowed by Ionic columns. The property around it is covered in snow, and I can't see another house in sight.

"Wow."

Jensen sighs. "Yep."

We get out of his car and walk up the slate-covered steps to the entrance. I wait for Jensen to let us in, but he rings the bell.

A few seconds later, the door swings open to reveal a middle-aged woman with a severe bun, a gray button-up blouse and matching skirt.

"Mrs. Keyes," Jensen says.

She opens the door further and ushers us inside. "Oh, good," she whispers. "You're here. Your mother was wondering what was taking so long."

Jensen gives Mrs. Keyes a quick hug. "I spoke with her less than an hour ago," he says quietly.

Mrs. Keyes shrugs. "You know how it is. And you must be Lucy." She's still whispering and I don't really understand why.

"Yes," I say. "It's nice to meet you." We shake hands and then she takes our coats.

The entry way is as large as you would expect after seeing the outside. The floors are tiled, the ceiling is vaulted and the walls are wainscoted and golden.

"You better get to the parlor," she says, shooing us down the hall.

Jensen takes my hand.

"Who is she?" I ask.

"The housekeeper."

"Oh."

Then Jensen is pulling me through an open doorway into what must be the parlor. It's a large open room with pristine white furniture, dark wood tables, expensive-looking rugs, and a bar in the corner.

"Darling, you made it," a woman at the bar says. She must be Jensen's mom. Her hair is short and blonde. She's wearing slacks with a cashmere sweater and pearls. She comes over and kisses Jensen on both cheeks, causing him to release my hand.

"Mom, this is Lucy," he says.

Her eyes meet mine before flickering up and down my body.

"It's nice to meet you, Mrs. Walker," I say, holding out my hand.

She takes it gingerly, setting her fingers in mine. I try to shake her hand, but then she slips it out of my grasp.

"Lucy." Jensen's dad approaches from behind Mrs. Walker. "It's nice to see you again." We shake hands, the motion much more comfortable than whatever occurred with Jensen's mother. He's wearing slacks like Jensen's, and a sweater over a button-up shirt.

"Would either of you care for a drink?" he asks.

They both have champagne glasses full of something.

"No thank you," I say.

Jensen takes my hand again and we sit on the couch. His parents each sit in a chair opposite us.

It's quiet in the room except for the ticking of a large clock behind Mrs. Walker's head.

"So, Lucy," she says. "My husband tells me you're part of the science department."

"Yes, ma'am."

"Please, don't call me ma'am. It makes me feel old." She smiles at me, but it doesn't touch her eyes. "You can call me Cynthia."

"Okay. Cynthia." I nod.

"What are you working on now?" she asks, before taking a sip of her champagne.

"I received a grant to study emotion as a pathogen."

"How interesting. How are you planning on doing that?"

I glance over at Jensen. He offers me a small smile and squeezes my hand.

"I'm working on developing a viable hypothesis," I say.

"Oh," she says.

The sound of the ticking clock infiltrates the space for a stilted moment while Jensen's parents both take a drink out of their glasses.

"How are you classes going, Jensen?" Professor Walker asks his son. "I hope you're devoting the necessary amount of time into catching up."

"They're fine," Jensen answers quickly.

We lapse into yet another silence. Before the silence has a chance to extend into an unacceptable length, Mrs. Keyes appears in the doorway.

"Brunch is ready," she says.

We file into the impressive dining room. The table is approximately the same size as my kitchen.

Plates are already laid out for us. I half expect a bevy of footmen in powdered wigs to appear.

Professor Walker sits at the head of the table, his wife on his right, Jensen at his left, and my plate is positioned an arm's length away from Cynthia's plate.

The housekeeper reappears with bowls of steaming food, and she proceeds to serve each of us freshly cooked eggs. It

144

feels odd, having someone dish out my meal for me but I stay silent, feeling more out of my depth than I would have expected.

Once Mrs. Keyes leaves the room, and we start eating, Cynthia turns to me.

"So. Lucy. Tell me about your family."

I finish chewing the food I put in my mouth and answer. "What would you like to know about them?"

"What do your parents do?"

"Mom," Jensen says, a warning in his voice.

I glance over at him and he gives me a slight grimace.

"What?" Cynthia asks him. "I just want to know more about your friend."

"My father owns the tire store on Ninth Street," I say.

"Oh. That's the discount tire place, isn't it?" she asks.

I nod.

"What about your mother?"

"My mom does a variety of things, from helping my dad with the bookkeeping, to making quilts and selling them on Etsy."

"On what?" Professor Walker asks.

"Etsy. It's an online store where individuals can market and sell various items."

I take another bite of my eggs while silence stretches yet again.

The conversation continues in this way throughout the rest of the meal, broken and quiet. I have no idea what to say to make them comfortable, but from the looks I receive from Jensen, I have a feeling most of their time together is this way, whether I'm there or not.

After the meal, I try to help Mrs. Keyes take the dishes to the kitchen—it's what my family would do, after all—but she insists I stay seated, and I get an almost panicked look from Cynthia when the words leave my lips, as if I had asked to dance naked on the table instead of trying to help perform the most menial of tasks.

"Well," Jensen says, after that moment passes. "We better get going. I have studying and a paper to get done before tomorrow."

We exit the dining room and head towards the door, his parents following behind us.

"Before you leave," Professor Walker says to Jensen, "I want to show you something in my study."

"Oh. Okay," Jensen says to him, and then he turns to me. "I'll be right back."

They disappear down the hall and I'm left in the foyer with Cynthia.

"Thank you for breakfast," I say after a moment. "It was delicious."

She nods and watches me in silence.

"How did you and Jensen meet?" she asks after a moment.

"We live next door to each other."

"Yes. He's lived there for nearly a year. He never mentioned you until recently."

"We didn't start speaking until recently."

"Why is that?"

"He's helping me with my experiment."

"Ah," she says, crossing her arms over her chest. "You're not good enough for him, you know."

I'm not sure how to respond to this, or if I'm meant to respond to this.

"It's admirable that you care so much for your son," I say, finally. "But I think he's old enough to decide what's best for him."

Her eyebrows lift at my words, and I'm amazed she's able to perform such a feat without causing nary a wrinkle.

We're both silent for another long moment.

"I better go see what's keeping Jensen," I say. I head down the hall in the direction they left in, half surprised Mrs. Walker doesn't attack me from behind as I move away.

There's too many doors to choose from. I find another bathroom, a storage closet that could be a room, and a room that looks nearly identical to the parlor. I finally stop when I hear the murmur of voices from a slightly open doorway.

"I don't want this to distract you from your schoolwork. You're already behind." I hear Professor Walker say.

"I'm catching up."

"But once you fall in the hole, it's easier to get buried. You really have to stay on it."

"It'll be fine."

"That means no distractions."

"I get it." Jensen's voice is clipped and low.

I knock gently on the door and then push it open further.

146

"Are you ready?" I ask.

"Am I ever," he mutters as he passes me, not bothering to say anything further to his father.

"Goodbye, Professor Walker," I say. "It was nice to see you again."

At this point, I'm not sure the sentiment is honest, but I'm unable to forgo the basic rules of politeness.

He nods and turns away without saying anything further.

Chapter Twenty

The heart has its reasons of which reason knows nothing.

—Blaise Pascal

"I am so sorry," Jensen says, for the fourth time since we left his parent's house.

"It's not your fault." We're almost back to the duplex. After our hasty departure, Jensen was silent for approximately five minutes before he began the effusive apologies.

"I brought you into the lion's den," he says. "I knew they would be difficult, they always are, but I didn't think they would be that crazy." He laughs. "If anything, I thought they would behave more if you were there as a buffer."

"You can't control other people's behavior. You can only control your own."

"I shouldn't have even told them we were—" He stops speaking suddenly and waves his hand, "Hanging out," he says finally.

He turns down the alley and into the parking spot, leaving the car on so the soft filter of music is still trickling through the air. Neither of us moves to leave the car right away.

"I hope I'm not distracting you from your studies," I say. "If you need assistance or if you want me to help in some way?"

"No. It's fine." He smiles at me. "What are you doing later?" he asks.

I pause at the sudden shift in conversation. "Freya is back, and she invited me over for dinner," I say. "I would ask you to come, but I'm not sure what the proper etiquette would be in this situation since it's at her house."

"Don't worry about it," he says. There's a pause and then he says, "Will you come over after?"

"Yes," I respond quickly. "I'm not sure how late it will be."

"That's okay." He shuts the car off then, and pulls the keys from the ignition. After fumbling with the ring for a moment, he hands a key to me. "Just let yourself in if I'm sleeping."

"Okay."

He gets out of the car then, and so do I, slipping the key in my front pocket.

We walk up the steps to the front porch in silence.

"Thank you for inviting me to brunch," I say, turning towards him.

When I look up, he's watching me with dark, serious eyes.

He reaches a hand out and cups my jawline. His thumb moves back and forth across my cheek. We don't do more than stare at each other for a few long moments. Then his hand exerts a gentle pressure, pulling me towards him. When our lips meet, it happens again. I try to maintain my composure, but something about the feel of his lips moving softly against mine and the smell of his cologne makes my normally active brain turn into a whirl of nothing but sensation and instinct. I slide my hands under his jacket and around his back, pulling our bodies together so we are touching from our chests down.

He pulls away and gazes down at me, his hands still on my face. "I should go," he says.

"Okay," I say.

Then he tugs me back towards him and this time the kiss isn't gentle at all. When we separate again we're both breathing heavily.

"This time, I really mean it," he says.

"Right," I say, leaning into him and pulling his head down towards me.

After a few moments, he removes his hands from me and takes a large step away. "Okay," he says. "I'll see you later."

I nod and turn away to head to my side of the duplex, but he grabs my arm and reels me in one last time. His kiss is hard and swift and then it's over and he's slipping back into his place.

It takes me a second to recover, and when I finally get behind my door I have to lean back against it to catch my breath.

***

I arrive at Freya's right at six o'clock, the time she told me to arrive.

She opens the door and reels me in for a big hug before pulling back and examining me from head to toe and then back to my face again.

"You look different," she says.

"I do?"

"Come in and tell us about your holiday!" She yanks me into the living room.

Ted and Bethany are already there, sitting on the couches and drinking wine. There's food on the coffee table: quiches, fruit, crackers and cheese. Her apartment is decorated with vintage items. The furniture is brightly colored orange and yellow hues, and she has a chair embroidered with floppy flowers. White fairy lights twinkle as they wrap around the room at the top of the walls.

"My darling genius girl!" Ted stands up and kisses me on the cheek.

Bethany stands too and gives me a hug. "You look different," she says.

I glance over at Freya. "Why are you both saying that?" I ask.

"Oh, yeah," Ted says, taking his seat back on the couch. "You've got this whole glowy thing going on." He nods solemnly and waves around his face with his hand.

"I do?"

"Yes!" Freya says.

We all sit down. Bethany and Ted plop on the couch, I sit on the flowery chair.

Freya sits on the floor and grabs a quiche to stuff in her mouth. "You had sex, didn't you!" she accuses around a mouthful of food.

"No," I say. "And not for lack of trying."

"OMG, I knew it!" Ted says. "You want to bone Jensen down, don't you?"

"I'm not sure what that means," I say. "But we have spent a lot of time together this week."

"You have to tell us everything!" Bethany says.

I tell them nearly everything, though I skip some of the more personal details and completely leave out the part about Jensen's artwork and the whole virgin thing. I get the feeling he doesn't share that last bit often. Or ever.

"Let me get this straight," Ted says, his face a picture of disbelief. "You've slept in the same bed nearly every night for almost a week?"

"Yes."

"And nothing happened?"

"Yes."

He claps his hands and his eyes turn gleeful. "Maybe he is gay!"

"No. He's not," I say assuredly.

"Well, are you guys together?" Bethany asks.

That makes me pause. "I don't know."

"Have you had *the talk*?" Freya asks.

"What's that?"

They exchange knowing looks.

Freya answers. "The talk about being exclusive. The one I never had with Cameron and then he ended up in bed with Liz the slut." She offers me a pointed look.

"No," I answer. "We haven't had that talk. But that's okay. I'm enjoying our time together."

"But you're not having sex?" Ted still appears confused.

"No."

"Hmph." He sips his wine.

"Tell me about your Thanksgivings," I say, in an effort to change the subject.

Freya talks about a former boyfriend she ran into in her hometown, Bethany complains about her grandmother's arbitrary and frequent use of moth balls, and Ted goes on and on about how his family played football and went off-roading.

Freya serves salad and lasagna and we eat in the living room. After dinner, there's more talking and laughing and then I'm ready to go home. Or to Jensen's home, rather.

"Thank you for having me over," I tell Freya as I'm leaving.

"No problem," she says, giving me a hug. "We'll get together for lunch this week?"

"Sure."

By the time I get to Jensen's it's after ten and all of the lights are off on his side of the duplex. I sneak in quietly using the key he gave me, leaving it next to the wabi-sabi dish in the living room before brushing my teeth with the toothbrush I've left there and crawling into bed with him.

He snuffles in his sleep, making me smile. I try and relax on my side of the soft bed, but for some reason I can't. After a minute of tossing and turning, Jensen shifts towards me and yanks me against him, one of his arms over my midsection and a heavy leg over mine. Once I'm pressed against him, feeling his body warmth seep into my back, it's easier to relax and before I know it I fall asleep.

***

The next day is Monday. Jensen has classes all day, and I spend the day staring blankly at my computer screen, still unable to reach the idea from the recesses of my mind for a viable experiment. Since sitting around doesn't seem to be effective, I decide to take a walk, hoping the increased blood flow and moving through the chilled air will shake something loose in my mind.

I'm heading home, still no closer to an idea, when my phone rings.

"Hey!" Freya yells into my ear. "What are you doing?" Her voice is a little anxious.

"Walking home from the lab. You?"

It sounds like she's outside. "I'm just now leaving the law library. Had a study group. Listen, I have to talk to you, can you meet me now?"

"I'm almost home and you're on the other side of campus. Are you okay? Can you tell me what's wrong?"

"Nothing's wrong," she says quickly. "It's just...ah...dammit." She pauses and huffs out a breath. "I didn't want to tell you this on the phone, but I saw Jensen with another girl," she says the last four words quickly, like ripping off a Band-Aid.

I stop walking and watch my breath come out in puffs in front of my face for a second. "So?" I ask. "He's allowed to hang out with people other than me, Freya. I don't expect him not to have other girls in his life who are friends. In fact, I've met some of his friends that are girls."

"It's not like that," she says. "I saw him hugging a girl. And they were pressed pretty close together and it seemed a bit more than friendly." She sighs. "I just had to tell you. I know you and Jensen haven't talked about being exclusive and I don't want you to get hurt."

"I won't," I say.

"How do you know?"

"What did she look like?" I ask.

"Blonde, legs up to here, basically your perfect bitch."

That sounds like Candice.

"That sounds like a girl I know he's friends with," I say.

"Okay, that's not all I have to tell you." Her voice is pained. "They walked off together and I sort of followed them."

"Freya!"

"I know, I know, but I couldn't help it. And...they went back to his place."

I'm not surprised. Jensen texted earlier and he had mentioned working on Candice's piece in between classes. I am surprised Freya took the time to follow him on my behalf. It's actually sort of sweet, in a terribly misplaced way.

Freya is still speaking. "I don't know how long they were in there together," she says. "I had to go because mob boss guy caught me hiding in the bushes, but it was longer than twenty minutes for sure."

"Does mob boss guy have an actual name?"

"Yeah. I think it's like, Dean, or something. He has this awful habit of catching me at my worst. My ass was literally sticking up and out of this bush when he came up behind me. At first, all I saw was his feet, then when I tried to back out, my hair got caught on a branch. He had to help me get untangled, and by the time that was finished, I had to run to get to my criminal law class."

"I think he likes you," I say. Why else would he stop and help her?

"What? No. He definitely does not like me. He's perpetually grumpy in my presence and he thinks I'm a dumbass."

"How do you know what he thinks?"

"You should have seen the look on his face when I told him I had criminal law! He was all, 'Isn't that a little advanced for you?' I almost decked him and then...wait! You're trying to change the subject and deflect attention from Jensen, but it won't work with me, missy."

"Freya," I say. "It's okay. They didn't do anything."

"How do you know?"

"I can't tell you. I just do."

"Listen, Lucy, no one disputes that you're a genius, but when it comes to stuff like this, you have to trust me. This guy is no good. And yeah, I mean, he's really hot and everything, but he's obviously damaged from what happened with Chloe and he's using this time to take advantage of you and who knows how many other girls."

"Freya, I know they didn't do anything."

"How can you possibly know that? You weren't there." She lets out an angry groan. "I can't believe that guy, acting all sweet and shit and the whole time he's totally playing you. Well, he's going to pay, believe you me."

"Freya, no," I say. I know exactly what she's thinking. "You cannot hire your mob boss guy to beat up Jensen, I won't let you."

"You can't stop me! Maybe I can get him to make a recorded confession, that way you'll believe me."

"Freya!" I sigh. I'm standing on the sidewalk alone. The campus is empty this late at night. I have visions of Jensen strapped to a chair and being coerced into a fake confession. "You know, a confession received under duress isn't admissible in court."

"Duh," Freya says. "But this is for your own good. And trust me, once you realize what an ass he is, you'll be glad of the bloodshed. Imagine him writhing in pain. It's not much, but it will keep you happy on those cold, lonely nights."

I run through my options in my head. I could continue to impress upon her that her proposed actions are unnecessary, but knowing Freya, that won't make much of a difference. Likely she needs something like this to latch onto to help divert her thoughts from the horrible experiences she had with Cameron.

"Listen, Freya," I say, finally. "If I tell you something, you have to promise not to repeat it to anyone."

154

"What are you talking about?"

Quickly, I tell her about Jensen's art, how Candice is involved, and how his dad would react if he found out. I realize while I'm telling her that I'll have to let Jensen know I've spilled. He asked me not to say anything, but surely, once I explain what Freya saw and how she was going to have him maimed in some way, he will understand.

When I finish, Freya is silent. All I hear is her breathing down the line and then, "Holy shit."

"Something to that effect, yes."

"Wow. I can't believe it. Man, I am so glad I was wrong about him! And don't worry, I won't say anything to anyone, I swear to god! I'm really happy that you're happy. And that I don't have to have him beat up now."

I laugh a little. "Me too."

"You should really have the talk with him. Tonight. Get it all out there, make sure he knows you're together and exclusive and all that stuff."

"I don't know," I say, mostly because I'm not really sure what such a talk would entail.

"You should initiate it!" Freya bursts out.

"What do I say?"

"Do it in your socially awkward, confusing way. He seems to like that."

"Okay."

We hang up and quicken my pace to get home. My mind has already moved ten steps ahead, and I nervously focus on the night ahead and *the talk*. I have no idea what I'm going to say, but that's never stopped me before.

Chapter Twenty-One

You'll never forget your first lover so try to make it someone you won't regret thinking about.

—Dr. Ruth

"Are you okay?" Jensen asks me when we're doing dishes after dinner. He had a meal of salad, roast chicken and potatoes waiting for me when I got home. Home to his house, not mine.

"Yes. Why?"

"You were quiet during dinner," he says. "Something on your mind?"

He shuts the dishwasher and pushes some buttons to start it before I answer.

"Yes," I say finally.

"Well." He takes my hand and leads me to the living room couch. "What is it?" he asks once we are seated.

He's still holding my hand and I look down at our linked fingers.

May as well jump right into the fire. "Are we exclusive?" I ask.

I lift my gaze to his and I find him examining me closely. "Why are you asking me this?"

The fact he answered with a question makes me nervous. "Are you afraid to answer?" I ask. My mind starts racing. Maybe he doesn't want to be exclusive. Maybe after all that, Freya was right.

"Why would I be afraid?"

I sigh. "Are we going to keep asking each other questions or should one of us answer eventually?"

"Fine. You first."

"But I asked the first question."

"But your answer to my question will determine the answer to yours."

I consider the implications of that statement. "Fine. We seem to be participating in something akin to a romantic relationship, but I'm not aware of the boundaries of said relationship. In addition, I've never been in this type of situation before and I would prefer to have things out in the open and know exactly how to define...us."

He nods. "That's fair."

But then he doesn't say anything, he just looks at me and I think he's suppressing a smile and I begin to feel a bit of frustration burning around the edges.

"And?" I ask.

"And what?"

"You haven't answered my question."

"Lucy." He takes my hand that's still tied with his and lifts it to his mouth to kiss the inside of my palm before holding it to his chest. "I've shared all my secrets with you. We've practically lived together for the last six days. You met my evil parents. I've given you the key to my place, and you have your toothbrush here. What do you think that means?"

I think it through. "That you're needy and a little lazy?"

He laughs and slugs me gently in the shoulder with his free hand. "It means we better be exclusive or you need to tell me if there's some other guy whose ass I need to kick."

I feel the burn of a blush creeping up my neck. "Okay."

"Okay," he says. "Now come here and cuddle before you have to leave me."

Cuddle appears to be synonymous with make out and feel up because that's what we do for the next hour, lying on his couch and facing each other, working ourselves into a frenzy only to have Jensen pull away.

"You better go before I make you stay," he warns.

"I wouldn't mind." My body is screaming for more, but I don't want to pressure him.

"I have to get up early for class and I don't want to wake you up. But I wouldn't mind so much either." Those perfect lips move in and he kisses my nose. "Come on, I'll walk you home."

It's freezing outside, but he treads across the porch in his socks and waits while I unlock my door. I'm grateful for the cold air, hoping that it will calm my racing hormones and heated body. Once my door is open, I turn and he pecks me on the lips before giving me a tight hug.

"I'll see you tomorrow," he says.

I watch him get halfway across the porch before I turn and step inside. It feels colder in here than it did at Jensen's. The light from the porch filters in through the window on the door, enough for me to see, at least. I shrug out of my jacket in the near darkness and hang it up before kicking off my shoes and shoving them in the closet by the door. I start heading down the hall towards the bathroom when there's a knock at the door making me head back and open it again.

It's Jensen. Standing there much like he was that first time a few weeks ago when I locked him out of his house. Hands in pockets, leaning back on his heels.

"Hey," he says.

"Hey," I return.

And before I can say anything else, ask why he's come back or what's going on, he's taken a few rapid steps in my direction. His arms surround me and he lifts me up, kicking the door shut behind him and pressing my back against the wall while kissing me like we didn't just finish a two-hour make-out session.

My blood, already heated and barely cooled down, immediately fires through my body and I wrap my legs around his waist, arching against him and hardly caring if I'm too heavy or if it will be even harder to let him go when he invariably puts a halt to the proceedings and leaves me again.

But apparently I don't have to worry about any of that because he carries me, wrapped around him, still kissing, down the hall stumbling through the dark and running his shoulder into the wall twice before getting to the bedroom. He sets me down on the edge of the bed. A sliver of moonlight filters through the thin curtains into the room, enough for me to see the heat in his eyes and the tension in his body.

"I can't wait anymore," he says, tugging his shirt over his head and throwing it somewhere behind him before reaching towards me.

158

I scoot back on the bed and he crawls towards me, eyes full of intent.

"Thank god," I manage before he's on me, kissing my mouth, nipping at my neck, and then pulling my shirt over my head and disposing of my bra within seconds.

We still have our pants on but the feeling of his bare chest rubbing against mine is enough to make me moan into his mouth.

He pulls back and watches me in the moonlight, cupping my face in his hands. "You are so beautiful," he says quietly.

"So are you," I say.

"I'm sorry," he whispers.

"Why?"

"This isn't going to take very long and it might be disappointing."

"I doubt that."

He chuckles a bit and leans forward, kissing me gently on the lips.

We help each other pull off the rest of our clothes and then we're skin to skin everywhere, lying on our sides facing each other. Our mouths meld, his tongue stroking into my mouth while his hands do wicked things between my legs, and within seconds I've lost all coherent thought.

"Do you have any condoms?" he asks against my throat.

"No," I say.

He curses and my brain wakes up a little. "There's no need," I assure him. "I've been on birth control since I was sixteen due to an irregular menstrual cycle. Plus, condoms are only eighty percent effective while birth control is ninety-nine percent effective against preventing pregnancy. Besides, neither condoms nor birth control protect you from sexually transmitted diseases. I can assure you that I'm clean," I say. "I've been tested and I have the results on file if you would like to review them?"

His head drops to my shoulder and he starts shaking with laughter.

"Is that humorous?" I ask.

He lifts his head to meet my eyes. "Yes," he says, his deep voice laced with humor. "It's funny because you talk like that and it shouldn't be hot, but it is." And then he takes my mouth with his again.

159

Everything swirls into sensation, my hands roving over his body, his hands playing my body like an instrument until finally he's settled between my legs and I can feel him sliding against me with a gentle pressure that's making me crazy.

I've never felt so out of control before. I want him so badly and I want him now, and I feel like he's intentionally driving me to frustration. We're still kissing as he slides against me, up and down, teasing me further until I arch against him and moan his name.

He pulls his face back from mine, holding himself up with his arms to look into my eyes and then with a slow stroke he's inside of me. Once fully seated, he stills and watches my face.

"Are you okay?" he asks after a minute of clutching each other in the most intimate embrace ever.

"Yes," I say.

"I was a little worried since I know it's been awhile for you, and you only had the one partner—"

"Oh, no, it's fine," I assure him. "He was very well-endowed."

His brows push together slightly. "What?"

"It was quite uncomfortable. This is much more manageable."

His mouth pops open and a noise that's a cross between a groan and a laugh emerges. "This is much more manageable?" he repeats in a strangled voice.

"Yes."

"As opposed to your science club lover who was, apparently, the size of a horse?"

I nod.

He throws his head back and laughs before leaning into me and resting his forehead on my shoulder, still shaking with laughter.

"Is it normal to laugh this much during intercourse?" I wonder out loud.

"Normal is underrated," he says, his breath fanning out against my collar bone. He pulls back to look into my face.

"I have to tell you, though," he says. "If there was anything you could have said to encourage me to make this the best time you've ever had, that was it."

I shake my head at him. "You males and your propensity for competition."

160

"I wouldn't knock that inclination if I were you. As a matter of fact, if you were smart you would encourage it."

"I would?"

"You might find the results satisfactory."

We grin at each other like fools.

After a moment, he moves slightly against me.

In response, I wiggle underneath him and run my hands down his body, encouraging him to move. Our smiles falter as passion overtakes our humor.

With a groan he complies, but slowly. Oh so slowly pumping in and out, teasing me again, making me squirm and pant and attempt to make him move quicker but he doesn't, and I reach a point where I think I can't possibly take it anymore. He's still holding himself above me, watching me get more and more turned on by his movements, his eyes getting more and more heated. I squirm underneath him, rising up to meet his slow thrusts, pulling at him and trying to make him go harder, faster. Then without warning he changes the angle and slams into me hard. Once, twice, and I'm quaking and shaking underneath him as an intense orgasm rips through my body, making my eyes shut of their own accord. When I open them again, it's just in time to see him shudder and moan and then his eyes close and his head drops to my shoulder as his own release races through him.

We lie there, panting, sweating, and boneless for a few minutes before he rolls off and gathers me against him.

"Wow," I say against his chest.

"Yeah," he agrees, running his hand lightly over my back. "That was..." instead of finishing the sentence with words, he chuckles softly and tightens his hold across my back.

"Yeah," I say.

After a minute, we clean up in the bathroom, both of us naked and I take a moment to appreciate Jensen in the bright lighting.

He's muscular in all the right places without being overly so and that part of him that was inside me only minutes ago is beginning to stiffen again.

He catches me staring and looks down at himself before returning his gaze to mine with a small smile. "I can't help it," he says. "You realize I'm in a near constant state of arousal when you're around."

That makes me smile. "Really?" I ask. We finish in the bathroom and head back into the darkened bedroom.

"Really," he says, sliding into the bed.

I get in on the other side and we move towards each other, meeting in the middle, his arms wrapped around me from behind and something hard poking into my back.

"Ever since the very beginning?" I ask. "When we first met?"

"Hmmm. I think it started when I saw you with that handlebar mustache."

I gasp in feigned surprise. "Ted's right, you are gay!"

He laughs, his chest rumbling against my back and he squeezes me a little tighter. "I think I've just unequivocally disproved those allegations."

"I'm not sure," I say, wiggling my rear against him. "I might need further proof."

The movement makes him suck in a quick breath. "Really?" he sounds surprised but intrigued.

I flip around to face him, grabbing him between the legs gently and rubbing him against me so he can feel how ready I am for him.

"Really," I say, nipping at his lips, and then I show him just how much he arouses me as well.

Chapter Twenty-Two

Should you shield the canyons from the windstorms you would never see the true beauty of their carvings.

—Elisabeth Kubler-Ross

When I wake up the next morning, Jensen is gone, and the sunlight is streaming through the windows.

Last night was amazing. I would have thought that experiencing so much pleasure in one night would result in a sudden withdrawal of serotonin or spontaneous combustion or something, but nope. I'm still intact and I still feel...happy. I have a vague memory of Jensen leaving earlier this morning, the brush of his lips on my forehead, a deep chuckle when I groaned and rolled away.

I smile. When he's happy, I'm happy. It's weird. It's like the closer we get, the more emotions we share.

I sit up in bed so suddenly I feel lightheaded.

"That's it," I say to my empty room.

I spring out of bed and rush to the closet to get dressed. I know exactly how I'm going to study emotions.

Two hours later, I'm sitting in front of Duncan in his office with pages of hastily scribbled notes.

"The hypothesis is that people who already share an emotional connection are more likely to feel the other person's impressions, even if the other person doesn't articulate the information to them. We can get two groups and split them into pairs; one group of couples who have been together for at least a few months. We could even break them into separate groups based on length of relationship to measure if the length of the relationship is a factor, and then have a control group of strangers. We incite emotions in one member of the couple, and ask how their partner feels. I'm willing to bet that the couples with established emotional connections are more likely to have the feelings transferred to them."

Duncan watches me with serious and appraising eyes. "That's a solid proposal."

I'm smiling like the Cheshire Cat, but I can't help it. I finally came up with something viable.

"How are you going to stimulate emotions in people?" he asks.

I bite my bottom lip. "I'm not sure yet. But I know I can do it."

He stands. "I know you can, too." He smiles at me. "Come back next Monday with some ideas, and we'll get to work."

I walk home in a daze. Everything is finally coming together. All I have to do is find a way to provoke people into an emotional state.

I'm definitely ready for a nap. Between the lack of sleep the night before and the excitement of the morning, I'm exhausted and drained. Jensen and I spent most of the night alternately sleeping, cuddling, talking, and doing lots of other things in positions that I never knew were possible.

Jensen is in class until the afternoon so I go straight home and fall into sheets that still smell like him.

A loud consistent banging wakes me up a few hours later. I glance at the clock on my way to the door, not quite awake, stumbling down the hall. It's not yet noon, and I wonder who it could be. I open the door without checking the peephole and Jensen is standing there, one arm leaned against my door frame, and he looks horrible. Not just tired from the night before, but upset and angry and I'm not sure what.

"Jensen," I say. I'm startled by his appearance and I immediately take a step towards him but he removes his hand from my door frame, and steps back and away from me.

"Are you okay?" I ask. I can't stop myself from reaching a hand out towards him, wanting to comfort him and erase the sadness from his eyes, but he avoids my hand, flinching away from me. My arm falls uselessly to my side.

"Who did you tell?" His voice is anguished, angry.

164

I blink at the sound of it and consider his question. I'm not sure what he's referring to, but the first thing that pops in my mind. "That we had intercourse last night? No one. I haven't talked to anyone since I—"

"No, Lucy." He shakes his head. "Who did you tell about my art?"

My stomach plummets. I can't quite believe we're having this conversation. I told Freya, but she would never break my trust. Would she?

I can't look at him. I stare down at my bare feet. They're getting cold on the linoleum next to the open door. I can't lie to him. I can't even make excuses. I did tell someone after I promised I wouldn't and the why makes no difference at this point.

"Freya," I say, hating the sound of my own voice.

He bangs his fist into the door frame, making me jump, and my heart rate accelerates even more, my breathing coming out faster beyond my control.

"Why?" His voice breaks on the word and I force myself to look up into his face. He's hurting and it's because of me. I did that to him.

I shake my head. "I have no acceptable excuses. I understand if you never wish to speak with me again."

"That's the understatement of the year. How could you?" It's almost as if he didn't hear me. I could shut the door, I suppose, and leave him at this point, but if it makes him feel just a little bit better to hurt me as I've hurt him, I will gladly take the verbal lashing.

"I understand that I'm nothing more than an experiment for you. A study to further your career, but this is my life," he says. He swallows and I watch his Adam's apple jerk with the movement.

He's wrong. I want to tell him he's wrong. He's so much more than an experiment, but then he's speaking again.

"My father called. They know the real reason I'm falling behind in my classes and they're cutting me off until I give it up. He actually drew up a contract that I have to sign, agreeing to his demands. Do you understand what this means? I can't go to school here anymore. I can't live here anymore. My life is over. Everything I want is finished. Everything I've worked so hard for is gone. Dust!"

I force myself to look at him. It's like I can see his heart breaking in his eyes, a reflection of the pain flashing in my chest.

"I trusted you," he says quietly. "I trusted you when I thought that I could never trust anyone ever again."

"I'm sorry," I say. The words are soft and inadequate.

"Not as sorry as I am." He shakes his head and then he turns abruptly and leaves, down the porch steps and to his car. I wait until he drives down the alley and I can no longer hear the sound of his motor before I shut the door, lean back against the cold wood and slide to the floor.

I can't believe that just happened.

I can't believe I messed up so badly. Why did I tell Freya? Who did she tell? The questions scatter in my brain when I realize one glaringly important truth. It doesn't matter. It's over. There's no going back now. The words can't be retrieved no matter how many times I think about. No matter how much I wish it could take it back. Why didn't I tell him when I had the opportunity? I meant to, but I was distracted by lust and Jensen and...it's no excuse.

A knock on the door wakes me up from my trance. I'm not sure how long I've been sitting on the cold, hard floor, but a significant amount of time must have passed because my butt is numb and my legs are tingling when I stand to open the door. I hope it's Jensen, but I'm sure it's not.

When I open the door, Freya is standing there.

"Are you okay?" she asks, pushing past me and into the living room. "I've been calling you all day! I saw Jensen in between classes this morning and he looked like a train wreck, what the hell happened?"

"He knows that I told you."

"Told me what?"

"The thing I told you not to tell anyone," I say quietly.

She wrinkles her nose. "How is that possible?"

"I don't know." I'm sad and frustrated and angry. The emotions are unfamiliar and confusing, which upsets me even more. It's like an itchy sweater that I can't remove because it's under my skin. "You tell me."

"I didn't tell anyone," she says.

"Then how did his parents find out?" I ask. "His dad...he's really angry."

"I don't know," she says. "Maybe someone else spilled. I'm sure people other than you and me know."

I shake my head. "Only a few people. One is out of the country and the others have known for a while and no one ever found out." I'm thinking of Candice and Anita, the art gallery owner. "I told you yesterday and today it's out. What am I supposed to believe?"

She puts her hands on her hips. "You don't trust me?"

"I don't know what to think." My voice is flat and emotionless. I cross my arms over my chest. "You should leave." I can't handle being around anyone right now. I step to the side.

She makes an annoyed sound and stalks past me.

"Fine," she says after she crosses the threshold.

And then she's gone and I'm alone.

A drop falls down my face and lands on the top of my foot. I bring a hand to my face.

I'm crying.

***

A few days pass in a blur of nothing. My mom calls a few times and so does Sam, but I don't have the energy to call them back. I don't eat much. I sleep a lot and by the end of the week, I'm sick of myself and my own overwhelming sadness. It's like nothing I've felt before. Everything that was so bright a few days ago now seems dull and lifeless and covered in a gray film.

Finally, I go to see Duncan at the clinic. I don't know who else to talk to, but for the first time in my life, I have the overwhelming urge to solicit assistance from someone else. I give him an abbreviated version of what I've been going through. I leave out the names of the people involved and anything involving me naked.

"Are you sure this girl is at fault here?" He's talking about Freya.

"Who else could it be?" I ask. "Logic dictates the simplest explanation is most often the correct one. I told her, his parents found out, it's the shortest line from A to B."

He steeples his fingers in front of his mouth and considers for a moment before saying, "Why don't you talk to her again, and this time assume she's being honest. Has she ever given you reason to believe she would lie?"

I think it over. "No, but I know she has withheld information from her friends before."

"That's not the same," he says. "This guy, he also unfairly assumed you had revealed his secret."

"But I did!"

"But you should never assume anything. Not if you want to maintain healthy relationships. We hear things about other people and we believe them, or we think we understand the motivation behind the behavior, but you will never really know unless you ask. If you don't know the whole story, you will make a mistake that you will regret. Ask the question. Always ask the question, never assume."

I nod slowly. "You're right," I say. "Thank you."

I get up to leave and I'm halfway to the door when he stops me.

"You'll be here and ready to work on Monday, right?"

I nod. "Yes. Thank you, Duncan."

"Don't thank me yet, we still have to get this thing going. But I'm sure you will."

I leave the clinic and head towards Freya's apartment, hoping she's home. It's ironic that this whole time, I've been trying to get my grant on track, and now that's done, it doesn't mean nearly as much to me as Jensen.

Freya answers the door in a dirty shirt and faded sweats, rumpled and frazzled.

"Are you okay?" I ask immediately. I've never seen her not put together and perfectly coiffed.

"Thank god you're here!" she exclaims, pulling me inside and shutting the door.

"Listen, Freya," I say. "I came over to apologize—"

"Shut up," she interrupts me. "Don't ever apologize to me for being emotional. I'm just glad you're really human, and not a cyborg like I've always thought. Now listen, I know I didn't tell anyone about Jensen. But someone did and I've been trying to find out who it was."

I stare at her in shock. "You've been trying to find out who told Jensen's parents about him?" I can't believe it. While I've been moping and crying, Freya's been proactively doing something. Why didn't I think of this?

"Yes, I figured, you know, if we find out who really did it, we can bring proof to Jensen and then he'll see and he'll forgive you and you'll be all hearts and roses and shit again. I haven't had a ton of success, but I have found—"

I throw my arms around her in a tight hug, and she stands there as still as a wooden post for a second before gently patting me on the back.

"Okay, Lucy." She pats me again. "Okay, you can let go now. It's starting to get weird."

I pull back. "Thank you," I say.

"No problem. So anyway, I found Chloe."

"Chloe? Jensen's ex-girlfriend Chloe?"

"Yes. *The* Chloe," she tells me with a wide grin. "And she's going to help us."

"Help us with what?"

She smacks me gently on the shoulder. "Help you get Jensen back, dummy."

I shake my head slowly. "I don't think that's going to happen."

I've been calling and texting Jensen numerous times over the last few days, but he never responded. Not that I expected him to, but I couldn't stop myself from trying.

"Oh ye of little faith," she says. "She should be here in about an hour. Come on." She walks into the living room and I follow. "Hang out while I'm getting ready. Use this." She hands me her MacBook.

"Use this for what?"

"I don't know, you're the genius. Follow some leads or something. Make some notes. Pretend you're a detective or some shit. Who else could have ratted Jensen out?"

I open the computer and start it up.

While she's showering I make a list of suspects. I include everyone I can think of who knows about Jensen's extracurricular activity, including myself and Freya, Chloe, Liam, Candice, and Anita.

Liam is out of the country and has been for weeks so I eliminate him as a potential suspect for the time being since I have no way to contact him, but maybe Chloe will have some insight when she gets here. That leaves Candice and Anita.

I don't know much about Candice – for example, something like her last name would be useful – but I do know a bit more about Anita, like I know she owns an art gallery and probably has electronic records stored somewhere.

"I have an idea," I say when Freya emerges from the bathroom. She's changed into jeans and a black long sleeve t-shirt. Her hair is still wet.

She sits on the couch next to me. "Oh yeah?"

"It's a long shot. And it involves breaking and entering." I shrug. "Perhaps violating a few privacy laws."

"Of course it does."

She doesn't seem terribly concerned.

There's a knock at the door and Freya stands to answer it. "She's early," she says, heading for the door.

I stay on the couch and listen.

"Hi, I'm Chloe, we talked on the phone?" I hear. She sounds a little nervous.

"Come in, Lucy's already here."

Chloe walks in and I can't help but check out the woman who broke Jensen's heart. She's watching me, too, and I wonder if she's thinking the same thing.

She's very petite, shorter and smaller than I am. Her wide blue eyes give her an air of innocence and frailty.

She sits on the couch next to me, where Freya was sitting only moments ago.

"Freya told me a little about you."

"Jensen told me a little about you," I respond.

"He did?" She seems surprised. "Was any of it good?"

"A surprising amount."

We engage in a brief staring contest. "Do you love him?" she asks suddenly.

"Yes," I answer without hesitation and I'm almost as surprised by my response as she is.

"No shit," Freya says. Apparently I've surprised her, too.

"Good." Chloe nods. "He needs someone who can appreciate him in all the ways I couldn't. Despite what you might think, I care about him a lot. Hurting him and breaking up with him, the way that it came about...it was the most shameful thing I've ever done and I will do anything to see him happy." She says the words with such conviction, I have to believe her.

I nod slowly.

170

"Well that's good," Freya says, clapping her hands together. "Even though this is probably the weirdest thing I've ever seen." She sits on the arm of the couch next to Chloe. "And I'm glad you're serious," she says to her. "Because apparently we're going to break some laws tonight. Now, who wants pizza?"

She orders the food and we go over my ideas and decide to break into the art gallery tonight. On nights when they don't have a showing, they close at eight.

"I'm sure they have a security system. How do we bypass that?" Chloe asks while we're eating. She was surprisingly excited once I outlined the plan.

"They do," I say. "I've been inside the gallery. Do you have any magnets on your fridge?" I ask Freya.

"Yes," she answers.

I nod. "Bring a few. We'll pick up the other supplies on the way."

Chapter Twenty-Three

After all, the ultimate goal of research is not objectivity, but truth.

−Helene Deutsch

After dinner, we raid Freya's closet. We dress warm and all in black including gloves, to avoid leaving fingerprints behind. Then, Chloe drives us over to Sam's and I run in and grab a few things. He's not home, but I have a key that he gave me for emergencies.

After Sam's, I have Chloe take me to an ATM and then we head downtown. I tell Chloe to park down the street from the gallery, and have them both stay in the car while I do a quick walk by. There are cameras above the front and back entrances.

Checking the angle of the camera as I walk by across the street from the gallery, I stop in the blind spot and pull out the paint gun I brought with me, borrowed from Sam. The streets are fairly empty this late. When there's no one around, I pull out my weapon and shoot at the lens. It takes two shots, but I finally hit it. I feel sort of guilty, but the paint will wash off and the camera will be good as new.

Once we're in the clear, I use the walkie-talkie—also borrowed from Sam—to let the girls know I'm ready. A few minutes later, they come slinking down the street. We head through a narrow alley on the side of the building and find a window. It's up higher than a normal window, and I'm glad. Most property owners won't arm a window that sits higher because it's more difficult to enter and they assume thieves will go for an easy entrance. We aren't thieves, but we are on a mission.

Chloe's the smallest one and I'm the tallest, so I boost her up to the window.

"You're totally grabbing her ass," Freya whispers loudly. "Is that weird? Groping your ex's ex?"

Chloe starts laughing and nearly loses her hold on the window sill.

"Freya! Not now!" I tell her.

Freya sticks her tongue out at me, and I turn away from her to check on Chloe's progress. She's trying to pull the window open.

"It's locked," she whispers loudly.

"Here," I hand her up the spark plug I took from Sam's garage. "Hit one of the panes with the porcelain side."

She complies and the small section of the window shatters. "Why was that so easy?"

"Simple physics. Now reach in, unlock it, and slide it open."

She's holding herself up slightly with one hand, so she has to open the large window one handed, but eventually she gets it done. Before she goes inside I hand her the magnet from Freya's fridge.

"We'll meet you at the front door," I tell her before hoisting her up and watching her shimmy inside.

A few minutes later we're in. The magnet was placed against the motion sensor on the door to trick the alarm and make it think the door's still closed.

Once inside, I lead them to the office, behind the door marked private.

I boot up the computer and Chloe and Freya start going through the files.

"Maybe she has a file on Jensen and someone else saw it and spilled," Freya says, pulling open a drawer and rifling through the paperwork.

The computer warms up and I head straight for the e-mails and personal files.

I find one from Jensen last week, letting her know he's headed out of town for the long weekend, but other than that...nothing.

"Did you guys find anything?" I ask.

"Nope," Chloe says.

"Not a goddamn thing," Freya says, shutting the drawer to the cabinet.

I shut down the computer. After digging in my pocket for the cash I retrieved from the ATM earlier, I leave it in a small pile on the window sill.

"That's why you needed cash?" Chloe asks.

"It's not right to break a window and not pay for it," I say.

"You're like Mother Theresa," Freya says.

"I don't think Mother Theresa ever broke into an art gallery in a misguided attempt to win back her boyfriend, whom she lied to and ruined his life," I say.

Chloe laughs and Freya grins at me.

I sigh. "Let's get out of here."

***

"Maybe we're going about this backwards," Chloe says.

It's the next morning. We're sitting in a corner booth at a little café not far from campus and we just finished ordering our food. After the unsuccessful misdemeanor committed last night, we had no idea what to do next and decided to meet for breakfast after a night of sleeping on it.

"What do you mean?" I ask.

"We're looking for who spilled the beans to Jensen's dad, and we're starting with the suspects," Chloe says.

"Yes, Captain Obvious," Freya says with a mocking salute. "So what?"

"Maybe we should start with Jensen's parents instead."

Freya and I look at each other and then I look back at Chloe. "You're right," I say.

"That actually makes sense," Freya says. "We could spend the rest of our lives searching for leads and find nothing. And then Lucy will never get laid again."

"Hey!" I object.

"If we work backwards, we might actually get somewhere. Chloe, you're a genius."

"Also," I add, "Professor Walker has a university e-mail so I can easily hack into that from my house and see what I can find."

174

"No more breaking and entering?" Chloe sounds almost disappointed.

I shrug. "Perhaps if the e-mail proves fruitless."

The food arrives. The waitress sets all our plates down and checks if we need anything before disappearing again.

"So tell me about this boyfriend of yours," Freya says to Chloe. "Liam?"

Chloe flushes slightly while squeezing ketchup on her eggs. "Yes?"

"You and Jensen were dating when you and Liam hooked up right?" Freya asks before stabbing a pancake with her fork.

"Freya," I say. "That might be a sensitive topic." I focus on Chloe. "You don't have to answer that."

"It's alright," she says. "Jensen and Liam have been best friends since high school. Liam transferred our junior year and they bonded over their art. I was with Jensen at the time, so we all hung out a lot."

"Liam's an artist too?" I ask before taking a bite of potatoes.

"No, musician and writer. But his parents weren't exactly supportive either; they would rather he get a real job." She pushes her food around her plate with her fork. "We've all been friends since then. Liam went travelling overseas as he likes to do." She smiles fondly. "After we graduated high school and when he came back, things were...different."

"Different how?" Freya asks.

"It's a long story, suffice it to say that Jensen and I had been growing apart for a long time and Liam," she pauses. "He challenged me. He helped me figure out who I am."

"That's nice," I tell her.

"Sounds like a bunch of bullshit," Freya says.

Chloe just laughs. "I would have said the same thing a year ago. Well, maybe I would have thought it, probably wouldn't have said it out loud."

"Why not?"

"I was...different, before Liam." She takes a big bite of food and that stops the questioning for the moment.

"So you guys hook up and he leaves the country? Doesn't that worry you?" Freya asks.

She shakes her head no. "He had the tickets purchased long before we got together and he's always had serious

175

wanderlust. He's coming back home next month and then I'm taking next semester off and we're going to Europe together."

"Where is he now?" I ask.

"Colombia," she says.

Freya finishes chewing a bite, wipes her mouth and throws her napkin on the table. "You don't worry about him hooking up with some Sophia Vergara look-alike?"

"No," Chloe answers immediately.

"Why not?" Freya sounds almost offended.

Chloe shrugs. "He picked me. And I trust him."

"Hmph," Freya says.

"Don't mind her," I tell Chloe. "She lacks confidence in romantic relationships due to prior abandonment and trust issues."

"No psychoanalyzing at the breakfast table," Freya says, picking up her napkin and tossing it at my head.

Chloe laughs.

Soon after breakfast we end up at my place with the laptop open on the coffee table in front of us.

They watch as I hack into the school's computer system and pull up Professor Walker's file.

"You are freaky good at this," Freya says.

I scan through the e-mails and read them quickly for anything relevant.

"There's nothing," I say finally.

"Does this mean we get to play ninja warriors again?" Freya asks.

"I don't know. We have no other leads."

We sit there, staring at the computer for a minute.

The silence is broken when Chloe's phone starts ringing.

"It's Liam!" she says, blue eyes lighting up and a wide smile making her whole face glow. She stands up from the couch, answering the phone and moving away from us, into the kitchen.

"Ugh." Freya throws herself back on the couch. "You people are disgusting."

"You'll fall in love again," I tell her, still staring at the computer screen and tapping gently on the keys, thinking.

"Not likely."

I can hear Chloe murmuring on the phone, still in the kitchen.

"No, he didn't go there for the holidays. There was a big storm and he got stuck here," I hear her say after a minute.

There's a beat of silence and then her voice escalates. "You did *what*?"

She runs out into the living room. "Guys," she says. "It was Liam."

Freya sits up. "What do you mean it was Liam?"

"He sent a card to Jensen's grandparents' house, thinking he would be there for the holidays. It was the orange head at a museum in Buenos Aires. And it said something about Jensen's art show?" she asks into the phone incredulously.

We watch as she listens to something he says and then she looks back at us. "It was in an envelope. His parents must have opened it," she says.

"Shitballs," Freya says.

"Definitely," I agree.

"You have to call him and tell him," Chloe says into the phone. There's a pause in the conversation and then, "It doesn't matter if he won't talk to you. Leave a message. Send a text. Or an e-mail. I don't really care, but you have to fix this!" She's silent while he's saying something and then she smiles, a glow lighting up her face. "I love you, too. Alright. Bye." She hangs up, still smiling, still glowing. "He'll take care of it, and he apologizes profusely," she says, sitting next to me on the couch.

I stare at the computer screen and after a moment I log out of the university system. "Now what?" I ask when that's done.

Chloe shrugs. "Now we wait."

My mind races with the possible consequences and variables of what could happen next. Or what might not happen next. "What if Liam tells him and it doesn't change anything?" I ask, voicing the thought that terrifies me the most.

Chloe puts a hand on mine. "Everything will work out," she tells me. "Don't give up hope."

Chapter Twenty-Four

Life is not easy for any of us. But what of that? We must have perseverance and above all confidence in ourselves. We must believe that we are gifted for something and that this thing must be obtained.

—Marie Curie

A week passes and I still don't see or hear from Jensen. Chloe tells me that Liam has done his due diligence, but he also hasn't spoken directly to him. I start to wonder if Jensen has disappeared off the face of the earth. If it wasn't for the fact that Chloe and Freya knew him too, I would wonder if he ever existed at all. It's like the time we had together was a figment of my imagination, or the most lucid dream ever.

I start work back at the department and it's going as well as can be expected. I definitely have more sympathy for the crying girls, and less panic attacks when people get emotional. We begin soliciting for interest in the study, and gathering a group of couples and singles for the different groups.

The rest of my life is strange. I've quickly made friends with Chloe. Freya seems to like her as well, despite Chloe's frequent soliloquies about how amazing love is and Freya's just as frequent gagging noises and suicide emulations. While I enjoy their company and humor, I can't help but feel like something is missing.

It's strange that I survived the first twenty years without Jensen in it, and he was only a part of my life for a few short months, but the lack of his presence is noticeable and startling. It's like a phantom pain. The limb is gone and I know it's gone, but the ache remains.

I'm walking home Friday night when I see a moving truck parked in front of the duplex. I stop and stare for a minute, heart pounding, breath coming out rapidly in the cold air, sending puffs of white out and up to the heavens, a smoke signal that no one will ever see.

What do I do? What do I say? Do I do anything? I'm struck with a sudden fear that if I see him and he speaks cruelly or simply ignores me, that something inside me will die and I'll never retrieve it.

When I get closer, I see people moving items around and into the truck, but none of them are Jensen. They're all strangers in uniforms boasting the name "Sanford's Movers."

There's a guy with a clipboard standing by the open end of the truck. He's wearing a dark blue long sleeve shirt with a name tag sewn over one breast. It says "Charlie". He's got a bushy mustache that's a bit longer down the sides and it reminds me of drinking Jenga night.

"Hello," I say as I approach.

"How ya doin' ma'am." He nods at me.

I stop next to him and watch a couple of guys carry Jensen's mattress out of the door and down the steps.

The thoughts of what happened on that mattress make me take a deep breath and swallow before asking, "Do you know if the former occupant is returning?"

"No, ma'am, I can't say I have that information."

"Can you tell me where you're taking these things?"

"No, ma'am." He shakes his head.

"Can you tell me anything?"

"No, ma'am."

"Okay," I say. "Thank you."

I'm not sure why I'm thanking him—he didn't help me in any way—but Charlie nods in acknowledgement and I wait until his guys are out of the way before I walk up the steps and back into my place.

I pull out my phone to call Jensen but it goes straight to voicemail. I'm like one of those girls that I used to advise to let it go and move on with their lives. I'm pathetic.

I call Freya.

"Hey poopies," she answers the phone.

"He's gone."

"What do you mean?"

"The movers are here. They're taking all his stuff out."

"I'll be right there." She hangs up before I can say anything else.

An hour later, Freya and Chloe are at the door, armed with bags of food and movies.

"I brought reinforcements," Freya says, motioning to Chloe.

"And I have some news," Chloe says.

They come in and put their bags in the kitchen before we return to the living room with bowls of food.

"Jensen's gone," Chloe says as we're sitting down. They put me in the middle of the small couch and they sit on either side.

"I know," I say. "I called Freya and told her—"

"No," she interrupts me. "He's not at his parents, either. They don't know where he is."

There's a pause while this information settles in. "What do you mean, they don't know where he is?"

"He was there and then he took off sometime yesterday and they haven't seen him since. They told my mom, and she told me when I called after I talked to Freya."

"The movers wouldn't tell me where they were taking his stuff," I tell them.

Chloe shakes her head. "That's not really his stuff. All of the furniture, all of his things, his dad bought for him. His dad's also the one who paid the movers to take everything out and put it in storage until 'Jensen comes to his senses.'" She finger quotes in the air. "At least that's what my mom said he said. And you might as well give up on calling his cell, his dad cut the service when they realized he was gone. He is completely off the grid."

Freya pats me on the knee. "Remember what you said to me, the first time we met?"

"I said a lot of things. None of which were useful."

"That's not true," she admonishes. "You said something about how letting someone else affect how you feel is handing over control of yourself to them."

"I'm an idiot."

"Shut up! It's true. Only you control how you feel and how you react to things. I'll admit, at the time I hated that you said that, but later when I thought about it, I realized you were right."

She moves closer and throws an arm over my shoulder.

"I know you don't want to hear this now," she says. "But it will all be okay."

"She's right," Chloe adds. "And we're here to help you through it. And so is Channing Tatum, Matthew McConaughey, and Joe Manganiello." She waves a DVD at me.

We watch the movie, and since it's not very plot-driven, I find myself watching Freya and Chloe's reactions to the movie more than the movie itself.

Once it's over, I ask them, "Do you find that you experience emotions when you watch movies?"

Freya shrugs. "Depends on the movie. But yeah, I guess so."

"*Steel Magnolias*," Chloe says. "When Julia Roberts dies. Makes me cry every time."

"*Braveheart*," Freya says. "I cry through, like, the whole thing. When his wife dies, when he's drawn and quartered at the end. Chills."

"Oh yeah!" Chloe agrees. "*The Notebook*," she says after a second.

"Yes!" Freya smacks her on the arm. "That one is so sad!"

"But Ryan Gosling is so hot," Chloe says.

"Totally."

My head moves back and forth between them as they talk. "That's it."

"That's what?"

"That's how I'm going to incite emotions in people. Make them watch movies that they find emotionally stimulating while they are in close proximity to their significant other. Or a stranger, for the control group. We'll have to put them somewhere where they can't see the other people, maybe with screened-in cubicles or small offices near each other. We can probably study proximity as well and how much of a factor that would be."

"Huh," Freya says. "Are you going to pay people to participate in this study?"

"Yes."

"You're going to pay people to watch movies. How do I jump on that gravy train?"

"I always cry in the beginning of *The Lion King* when Simba's dad dies," Chloe says.

"Right? Disney is so messed up with that stuff."

They continue discussing movies that make them cry, and I catalogue the information in my mind for future reference. I wish I could call Jensen and share the news with him. I never got a chance to tell him about my idea at all. The thought makes my chest hurt, but I can't do anything but keep moving forward.

Chapter Twenty-Five

The ultimate lesson all of us have to learn is unconditional love, which includes not only others but ourselves as well.

−Elisabeth Kubler-Ross

Another week passes and by the next Friday, I am feeling better about everything. The clinic work has gone better, and I'm developing relationships—therapist-client relationships—with some of the students.

The board approved our ideas and we've already begun purchasing supplies and finding an adequate location.

It's the end of the day. I'm the only one left in the entire clinic, and I've just finished my last client. I'm still in the patient room looking out the window at the quad, my hands on the sill, my forehead resting against the cold glass. There aren't many people outside, just a few walking from one building to the next, wrapping their coats around themselves and fighting against the wind.

I've gotten to the point where I'm sure I'll never see Jensen again. And if I do, it won't matter because he'll never forgive me and I'll never forgive myself. But I'm ready to move on. I'm happy with the person I'm becoming. I have friends. I have a job. I'm learning more and more about what I need to make me happy, and it doesn't necessarily involve a relationship.

There's a knock at the door behind me and I call, "Come in," without turning around or changing position.

The door shuts gently and then, "I was wondering if you're still seeing patients today?"

I immediately recognize the voice. My breath puffs out of my mouth, leaving a flat cloud against the glass. I spin around, leaning back against the window sill, needing something to hold on to.

"It depends," I answer more calmly than I feel.

"On?"

"What the patient needs."

Jensen moves into the room, his eyes never leaving mine, and sits on the couch. He looks good. Tired, but good. He's wearing the same stained brown shirt he was wearing the first time I knocked on his door, and old faded jeans.

Who was I kidding? I was never going to give up and move on. I might have lasted another week before I searched public records or his credit report to find out where he was living. But now, no stalking necessary. I almost can't believe he's here.

He takes a deep breath and leans forward, placing his elbows on his knees.

The only sound for a moment is the tick of the clock on the wall, and the thundering of my heart in my ears. Should I say something? Should I wait?

He bites his lip and runs his hands through his hair. A nervous gesture that's familiar to me. "I need to apologize," he says.

I'm surprised. He's apologizing to me? "For what?"

"I was wrong. I shouldn't have blamed you."

I'm not sure how to respond. Apology accepted? Then what? Will he leave? I don't want him to leave. I'm silent long enough that my opportunity to respond passes.

He continues. "No, that's not it. I mean, that's part of it, but remember when you told me that I was letting my dad dictate my life?"

I don't answer. Of course I remember. He knows I remember.

"You were right," he says. He looks away, his eyes focused on the ground somewhere in front of his feet. "I was living my life based on my parent's expectations, and hiding who I really was, but I'm not doing that anymore." He looks up and our eyes meet. "Anita sold a couple of my pieces. I used the money to move into a new apartment. I'm not going to take money from my parents any longer. I've been doing it for so long, I've

184

gotten so used to doing whatever they want and taking whatever they give, but not anymore. I'm ready to be my own person and do what I want and live on my own dime and on my own terms.

"My mother told me that you were using me for your experiment. When I asked how they found out, she said you told them about everything. Well, she didn't use those exact terms, but she didn't deny it either. She led me to believe you were just using me, and you wanted to hurt me to further your study. When I talked to Liam, I realized what had really happened."

I've moved in his direction without realizing it. I'm almost to the chair I always sit in during the sessions, across from the couch where he is.

I sit down in the chair and watch him expectantly.

"I dropped out of school," he says. "I'm going to go back, when I can afford it or when I can figure out how the whole student loan thing works. Until then, I'm going to live off of my art, and if that doesn't work, I'm going to get a job. But I'm never going to give up doing what I love."

"That's good. I'm glad." I really am. He deserves every bit of happiness, whether I'm part of that happiness or not.

He looks down at the couch, and his fingers fiddle with a bit of fabric that's come loose on the old piece of furniture.

"The thing is," he says quietly and then clears his throat. "The thing is," he repeats it louder. "I don't want to do any of that." His eyes meet mine again. "Without you."

My stomach drops and my heart accelerates. Is he saying what I think he's saying?

I can't speak. For the first time in my life, I'm speechless. But then, I'm not surprised, I've experienced a lot of firsts with Jensen.

Eyes still on mine, he gets off the couch and moves around the coffee table towards me. He approaches me slowly, like I'm a feral animal that might bolt if he makes any sudden moves. When he reaches my chair, he bends to his knees in front of me and puts his arms on either side of my legs. His hands rest against the outside of my thighs, and he places his head on my lap.

"I've missed you so much," he says. "At first I was so angry with you. And then I was angry at myself. And time kept passing, and the more time that passed the more ashamed I felt about my behavior and I realized what an idiot I was. I thought it was too late to get you back. Then I talked to Liam and the whole damn thing was even worse and—"

"Hey," I say, putting my hand on his head, still in my lap, and interrupting his tirade. "Wait."

He looks up at me and I can't help it, I run my hand through his hair and cup the back of his head.

"It's okay," I tell him. "You aren't the only one who screwed up. I may not have been the source of the information that leaked, but I did betray your trust."

"Liam told me how Freya threatened to use her hit man on me," Jensen says with a small smile.

"That doesn't make it okay. I should have told you. I meant to tell you right away, and then I was distracted by all the sex and your body and..." I trail off, not really sure how to continue that sentence.

"What do you say we call it even?" He's grinning up at me now.

I smile. "That sounds perfect."

He shakes his head. "Nothing in life is ever perfect."

"Well, it sounds perfectly imperfect."

He laughs—a deep chuckle that hits me somewhere in my chest—and then he moves up until he's sitting in my lap, making me laugh as his more considerable weight settles on top of me. My hands move from the back of his head to his shoulders.

He's squishing my legs, but I don't care. His hands cup my face, and he moves in until our lips are nearly touching, but not quite.

"Lucy," he says, the word tickling against my lips.

"Yes," my voice comes out rather breathlessly.

He pulls back slightly to look into my eyes. "I love you."

My hands flex against his shoulders and I nod. "I love you, too."

He smiles, a beautiful and blindingly wide flash of teeth, and then he's kissing me and I'm kissing him and I'm very glad everyone else has gone home for the night. Duncan said it was okay for me to lock up, and that's great because now I'm pulling at Jensen's shirt and tugging it over his head and his eyes meet mine, full of passion and desire and love.

"Are we christening your work place?" he asks.

"Call it whatever you need to," I say, making him laugh.

186

I push him off my lap to the floor and then I follow him down, sprawling on top of his now bare chest and kissing his neck.

"Lucy?" he says, sighing and pulling me up closer to his face. "Will you move in with me?"

I blink down at him. "Really?"

He grins and shrugs awkwardly. "I could use a roommate. I'm sort of a starving artist now."

"Okay," I say, and then he tugs me down towards him, kissing my mouth, then my cheek, then below my ear.

"Plus I kind of like having you around," he says against my neck.

"That's good," I respond.

"And just think about how often we can do this." He nibbles at my collarbone, and for a second I can't breathe.

"I'm not arguing," I tell him. "You really don't need to convince me."

"Oh, there is every need," he says.

And then he proceeds to show me just how wonderful our imperfect life will be.

Coming soon – Imperfectly Legal

Freya Morgan thought it was a great idea to hire the bad boy on campus to beat up her douchebag ex-boyfriend after he cheated on her and treated her like crap. Fast forward a few months, and now the bad boy she hired is in trouble. And it's sort of her fault. After all, if she hadn't hired him in the first place, she wouldn't have started the trend of all the ladies on campus paying him to do their dirty work. But now, those boys he's being paid to beat up are ending up dead, and he's the prime suspect and he expects Freya to help him find the real killer.

For Victims of Rape

Freya's situation is not uncommon. Over 60% of rapes go unreported and 97% of rapists never spend a day in jail (https://www.rainn.org/statistics).

If you or someone you know is a victim of sexual assault, I hope you will report, or encourage the victim to report. Even if you don't succeed, you may save a future victim.

Although Lucy may understand and articulate the "biological urges" of homo sapien males, as a species, we have evolved to the point where we can control our urges. No always means no, whether you are male or female, and whether you are with a friend, boyfriend, husband, someone you've slept with before, or someone you are fooling around with now. The choice to share your body is always yours.

For more information, you can contact RAINN (Rape, Abuse & Incest National Network) at www.rainn.org or their hotline at 1-800-656-HOPE.

Acknowledgements

First off, thank YOU beautiful reader for making it to the end of this book without tossing it aside in disdain and/or horror. I appreciate that you took a chance on an unknown writer, and I hope you enjoyed the story. For more information on what's coming next, you can find me at my blog: marewolf.blogspot.com, or on twitter: @marewulf

Thank you to my husband for dealing with me having my nose in my laptop or book for hours on end. Your unflagging encouragement and belief in my abilities astounds me. I love you.

My mother and early reader, Elizabeth Baines. Thank you for always believing I could do this, even when I was writing crappy stories with flat characters, and probably still am.

A giant squeeze and thank you to Mary Baader Kaley. I know you don't believe this, but without your knowledge and support, it would have been another five years before I wrote anything even remotely publishable. And if it weren't for you, I wouldn't know most of the people listed below.

My earliest beta readers who provided wonderful input: Jennifer Ortiz, Kirsty from Goodreads, Jenny Juchtzer, Maria Michel, Adrienne Leyland and the aforementioned Mary Baader Kaley.

My lovely goat readers: Angela Cook, Precy Larkins, Ashlee Supinger, Suzanne Payne, and Riognach Robinson. You guys amaze me! Plus, the rest of #TheGoatPosse I don't know what I would do without each and every one of you and your input and support.

And last, but definitely not least, this book would not be half as good as it is without Jenn Marie Thorne. Your ideas, encouragement, and gentle (or not so gentle, ha!) prodding made this book a bazillion times better than I could have done alone. Look for her debut novel, THE WRONG SIDE OF RIGHT, Spring 2015.

CPSIA information can be obtained at www.ICGtesting.com
Printed in the USA
LVOW06s1700230914

405475LV00006B/1003/P

9 781495 473181